AF148091

Souls Apart

(A Vision of Britain in the grip of Tyranny)

by

Lionel Ross

ISBN: 978-0-9567668-7-8

Souls Apart

(A Vision of Britain in the grip of Tyranny)

by

Lionel Ross

ISBN: 978-0-9567668-7-8

Published by

i2i Publishing. Manchester.
www.i2ipublishing.co.uk

Dedication:
To Luise: My constant inspiration

The people always have some champion whom they set over them and nurse into greatness. This and no other is the root from which a tyrant springs; when he first appears he is a protector.
Plato *(BC 427-BC 347) Greek philosopher.*

So long as men worship the Caesars and Napoleons, the Caesars and Napoleons will arise to make them miserable.
Aldous Huxley *(1894-1963) British author.*

Tyrants such as Hitler use democracy to give them power and then destroy it and all its institutions.
Lionel Ross *(1935-   ) British author.*

Author's Note:
This is only a story but never shelter behind the thought that it could not happen here.

By the same Author:

Fine Feathers 978-0-9552404-2-3

(Originally published by **PublishAmerica** 2005)

(i2i Publishing 2006)

Hidden Heritage 978-0-9552404-1-6

(i2i Publishing 2006)

The Baghdad Declaration 978-0-9552404-3-0

(i2i Publishing 2007)

Men of Conviction 978-0-9560369-3-3

(i2i Publishing 2009)

The Dalethorpe Chronicles 978-0-9560369-7-1

(i2i Publishing 2010)

CHAPTER ONE

BRIXTON

1969

It was a bitterly cold December night and Jack and Julie Rodgers were curled up on the large dralon velvet settee in front of the fire to watch the flickering images on their 12" Phillips television set. They had been married for sixteen years and life had been far from easy. They had a son Christopher, fourteen years old, a bright boy who had won a scholarship to the local grammar school and a daughter, Carol, nearly thirteen. She was less successful at school but her friendly nature and bright personality ensured her popularity among her friends and family.

It was over a year since Jack had told Julie that he had been made redundant as assistant manager at the supermarket on the high street. This, he said, was as a result of much of their business being lost to a huge competitor unit that had opened on a vacant plot nearby. At the time this blow had left them reliant on Julie's wage as a part-time cleaner.

Julie wondered if this was the real reason why Jack had lost his job but she knew better than to question him as this inevitably led to him flying into another of his rages.

Jack had never been an easy man and recently had become even more bad tempered and morose than hitherto. This Julie explained away to herself as frustration caused by his lack of employment. She always tried to make allowances for Jack's moods.

Their children were out for the evening visiting school friends. There had been the usual argument between Jack and Julie as to which TV programme to watch. Jack liked *Colditz* with its weekly stories of allied soldiers escaping from Nazi imprisonment whereas Julie was fascinated by the comings and goings in *Upstairs Downstairs*. This programme showed a way of life so completely different from hers that being immersed in it, even for an hour, constituted a complete escape from their constant financial struggle. As usual Jack's choice had prevailed. It had to be said that Julie also enjoyed *Colditz* whereas Jack had no patience with the romantic perambulations of the British upper class and their servants portrayed by *Upstairs Downstairs* in early twentieth century London.

On the TV, a small group of allied soldiers had just scaled the walls of the almost impregnable castle that acted as a detention camp for prisoners of war. The front-room of the Rodgers house was filled with the noise of shooting and shouting emanating from the TV set. Suddenly there was an ear splitting scream that initially seemed to attach itself to the cacophony.

"What the hell was that?" Jack asked.

"I think it came from the back entry," Julie whispered, looking pale-faced and somewhat shocked.

Jack jumped up from the settee and made his way, via the tiny kitchen, to the back door that led onto their yard. Julie followed him wondering who or what could be responsible for the scream. Jack undid the sliding bolt on the yard gate and peered anxiously up and down the dimly lit entry passage.

"Well there is no one out here," he pronounced grumpily and then he noticed what looked like a bundle of old clothes lying on the ground nearby. He walked towards it and as he did so he could hear the sound of heavy breathing; no it was more like panting, coming from the article he was about to investigate.

It was indeed a pile of clothing or more properly rags and lying on the rags, barely covered from the freezing cold by more rags, lay a young woman fighting for breath. Jack knelt down besides her.

"It's all right," he said in an uncharacteristically comforting voice.

He looked again at the barely conscious young woman and thought that the pain ridden and emaciated face looked vaguely familiar. He tried to speak again to the figure lying on the ground but she seemed incapable of speech. He then decided to call his wife.

"Julie," he called. "Come and help me! It's a young lass and she seems to be in a bad way."

Julie was approaching with a certain amount of trepidation when they both heard another sound.

"My God," Julie exclaimed in horror, "she's got a baby under there."

Julie whisked away the filthy cover and discovered a new-born baby boy crying lustily. She ran back to house to fetch a knife to cut the cord, still attached to the profusely bleeding mother. She picked up the naked infant and ran into their house to give the poor little mite, warmth and cover.

Jack tried to raise up the young mother but all her efforts were directed to her breathing. Then her body arched up and with a further ear-splitting scream similar to the one that had alerted them in the first place he realised that she was still undergoing the pangs of giving birth. As a mere man it had not occurred to him that another baby was on the way. He had accompanied Julie to the labour room when their children had been born but in those days it was more usual for the father to wait outside, pacing the floor, than to be present at the birth. Suddenly Jack realised what was going on and raised the cover over the girl's legs. And there it was, another baby. He had seen on the films that new born babies often had to be picked up and slapped on the buttocks to make them start to breathe. The baby was, of course still attached so he knelt down and picked up the little mite. A few moments later this baby was crying lustily. Jack put the baby down again and ran to the house to tell Julie that he would stay with the first baby while she went to cut the cord, collect the second child and see to the mother.

A minute later Julie was back with baby number two.

"You must get an ambulance," she instructed. "That poor young girl is bleeding badly and is very weak."

"Go to the phone box and dial 999," she instructed urgently. Only the relatively comfortably-off had telephones in their homes in those days.

Jack walked down the road and told the operator to send help at once.

Julie then told Jack to go back to the mother lying in the passage and see if there was anything he could do to help the poor girl until the ambulance arrived. As he approached her there was silence and kneeling down besides the now still body he realised that the young woman had expended the last breaths in her body to push the second twin into the world.

Ten minutes later the ambulance arrived and confirmed that after depositing two healthy baby boys into this often cruel world, the young woman had departed, hopefully for a better place.

She carried no identification and the ragged clothing she wore gave no clues to her origin. She seemed to be very young, probably eighteen or nineteen at the most. Her skin tone was just a little darker than Jack's and she had dark curly hair. In her pocket, the policeman who arrived at the same time as the ambulance found a purse. This contained just two of the new five pence coins that had recently replaced the old shillings and some odd pennies. The only other items were two identical metal charms which were often hung on bracelets when silver and gold were beyond the budget. These charms were in the shape of seven branch candelabrums.

The Rodgers were commended by the social services department for undoubtedly saving the lives of the two babies. They had to accept that the poor mother of the twins was too far gone to be saved and Jack and Julie had their five minutes of fame when the local paper interviewed them and published the story. This resulted in Jack being offered a position in the new supermarket and was some reward for all they had achieved that night.

Jack, much to his wife's amazement, wanted to adopt the babies. Julie however was insistent that in their current parlous financial state, this was out of the question. In the end Jack had to agree that it was taking all of their meagre resources to maintain themselves and their own children. It was normally very unusual for Julie to win an argument as she hated to cross Jack because of his foul temper.

The twin boys were taken into care until good homes could be found for them with adoptive parents who would love them and compensate for their terrible start in life.

Chapter Two

Belgravia - 2007

The Philipino man-servant had been told to expect fifteen guests, all gentlemen. As they arrived he checked their names on the list his master had provided and relieved them of their coats. Then he ushered them into the large dining room. The man was called Rupert and he had lived in England for some fifteen years. He was an avid follower of news and current affairs programmes on the TV set in the servants living quarters which he shared with his wife, Maria. That was, of course, when his master and mistress had no need of his services. He was both impressed and curious when he started to recognise a number of his master's guests as being prominent members of the political establishment. Obviously, as the soul of discretion, he showed on his face no flicker of recognition when the guests gave their names to him, to gain admittance.

His master, Colonel Sidney Charleston was a hero. He had returned from tours in Iraq and Afghanistan as one of the most decorated officers in the history of his most distinguished regiment. As he rose through the ranks he had personally performed a number of acts of conspicuous bravery that had earned him the gratitude of senior officers and of those junior to him. He could, however, hardly be described as a modest man and he lost no opportunity to recount his own triumphs and achievements to friends, his wife's family and colleagues. Now he had retired, or rather been invited to retire, as a result of the increasing celebrity status that he enjoyed at home. This he used to pontificate on many military and political events. The media loved him. He could always be relied upon for an opinion and as many of his public statements were inappropriate to have been articulated by a senior serving officer, he was gently and quietly relieved of his command. Because of his growing popularity with a vast number of members of the general public it was deemed to be unwise to publicly criticise him. Now, he realised, as a civilian, there would be no such restraints placed upon his utterances.

Sidney was tall and slim with what the media usually described as a 'Mediterranean' appearance. He was the only child of Bessie and Gerald Charleston and his parents had doted upon him. Gerald was a bank clerk and was still to found behind the counter, after thirty years and a career that was remarkable for its long service and diligence but which had failed to be recognised for promotion by reason of his lack-lustre personality. In the early days of their marriage, Bessie had worked as a shorthand copy typist in a solicitor's office but the increasing use of computers and her technophobic attitude to them had resulted in her retiring to become a full-time wife and mother to Gerald and Sidney.

Their son had surprised, nay amazed, all who knew the Charleston family by his sunny, outgoing personality and his determination and ability to pursue his school career. This culminated eventually in high grade 'A' levels in English, History and Geography. His headmaster at the Islington High

School, Roger Culshaw, had quickly realised Sidney's potential as a pupil of exceptional ability and had personally ensured that the staff gave the young man every facility to further his studies. Here was a pupil who would enhance the flagging reputation of the establishment. Roger's confidence in the boy's ability was eventually justified by a scholarship to Cambridge where his Studies in Political Science resulted in a First Class Honours Degree.

During his time at Cambridge he had formed a relationship with the glamorous blonde daughter of a successful stockbroker and soon after he received his degree, he was married to the young lady. Her name was Daphne Craigwell-Smyth and her parents were less than impressed with the match particularly after meeting Bessie and Gerald. Daphne, however, had always possessed a mind of her own and had been expelled from a well-known public-school at the tender age of thirteen for smoking cannabis. It was a profound relief to her parents that she had then settled down in another similar establishment and gained a place at a lesser-known Cambridge college. Her parents ever since that time, were constantly in dread of her 'going off the rails' again and gave in to her every whim.

"I have to say," Charles Craigwell-Smyth told his wife, "the boy is obviously very bright and if we don't agree to the marriage, Daphne will probably run off with the feller anyway. I wouldn't put it past her."

Soon after the marriage Sidney had discussed career possibilities with his wife and father-in-law and they all agreed that if he was not to go into the city, being an army officer would be an excellent launching-pad for whatever was to follow. As his military career had progressed, Sidney had made it his business to cultivate the friendship of those senior to him, both in rank and background. As a result he numbered among his friends many sons of the aristocracy and the political establishment. This gave him an entry into the homes of the major decision makers in the country and especially those who shared his increasingly right-wing view of the direction that the UK, USA and Western Europe should be taking. He was a natural leader of men and the cultivated upper-class drawl, which belied his humble origins, had assisted him in persuading his friends of the necessity of forming a new political party in the UK.

It was June 2007 and Tony Blair had just resigned as Prime Minister. Much to the horror of Sidney, who was certainly not a fan, Gordon Brown had taken over.

Charles Craigwell-Smyth had originally purchased a 'modest' Town House in Belgravia for the young couple where his daughter and two young grandsons lived whilst father was away on tours abroad. Now, with his army career over and back in full-time residence, Sidney resolved to gather around him a number of friends for an inaugural meeting of the Western Democratic League. This had been his dream for many years but he was a patient man and knew he must bide his time. The final prize would be so great that a very long wait would be justified for what was to be his ultimate goal but few could have realised what that eventual goal was.

As a result of his media fame, and no doubt with the active participation of his father-in-law, he had been offered and accepted a number of seats on the boards of public companies. Thus, with a more than comfortable income assured, he quickly became financially secure.

Sidney was no racist. Anyone who believed strongly in Sidney's often stated views of the way forward for western democracy would be able to join the WDL. Indeed, invited to the inaugural meeting were representatives of a number of 'establishment' ethnic organisations. These included Sir Carlos Thompson, an afro-Caribbean member of parliament on the right-wing of the Conservative party; Jacob Rothberg who was the chairman of the Jewish Council for Democracy, Sanjiv Joshi of the Hindu Defence League, Ahmed Yamani of the British Muslim Council Against Extremism and a number of prominent spokesmen for right-of-centre organisations representing all four of the constituent nations of the United Kingdom. Sidney was firmly against the divisive policies of the British National Party and the English Defence League who he claimed to regard as little better than ignorant thugs. The policy of his party was to be inclusivist. No-one would be excluded on racial or religious grounds.

Once everyone was seated around the long dining table, Sidney began,

"Gentlemen, none of you know why you are here and I thank you for having sufficient confidence in me and my motives to accept my invitation to attend. Most of you are acquainted with me personally and those of you, who are not, will no doubt be aware of my oft-expressed views when interviewed by the media."

Sidney paused and glanced quickly but searchingly at the facial expressions of his guests. Yes, he decided, he undoubtedly had their wholehearted attention.

"Before proceeding any further with what I have to say I require personal assurances from all of you that you will not disclose the subject of tonight's meeting to any living soul outside this room. That includes wives, close associates and in short everyone."

Once again he paused and this time fixed a penetrating stare on each of them in turn and in response received a re-assuring nod.

"Finally may I say that you are all at liberty to disagree with what I am about to say and if you feel strongly, you may leave at any point during my address and our subsequent discussions. Should you thus disassociate yourself, I will still require your promise of silence to be strictly honoured."

Again agreement was signalled by way of a nod.

"Well, gentlemen," Sidney continued, settling himself back in the comfortable dining chair. "How many of you are happy with the torrent of left-wing legislation that is being spewed out by Brussels? And for that matter how many of you are happy with the obsession of our lords and masters of the political establishment to be, what they call, politically correct?"

Sidney knew who he was talking to. He should have done; they were all personally selected by him and many had made similar pronouncements in recent times.

"Gentlemen, this has to stop. I propose to ask you to join a new political grouping, but one that must remain secret for the time being. I suggest we call it the Western Democratic League. And let me emphasise that our party, when the time is ripe, will be set fair to become not only the government of the United Kingdom but also to promote our ideas and ideals to all other Western nations. Unlike the small minded people of UKIP, I believe in Europe, but a very different Europe from the one we currently endure. Our job will be to change the direction of Europe from within, not from outside. Equally, although this is self-evident to everyone around this table, we are not a racist movement; I want to see right-thinking people from all races and religions active in our group. And finally may I say that when Europe is properly governed, we can turn our attention to the crumbling democracy of the USA."

The group expelled a collective gasp at this last statement but Sidney's carefully selected words were ringing true with the chosen assembly. How much of what he had said he really believed himself was debateable, but he was selling the idea of a new all-powerful political group and to do so he must tell his associates what he knew they wished to hear.

Sidney surveyed the faces in the room and as he had somewhat arrogantly expected, all the ensuing comments were positive.

Much was discussed on that fateful evening and finally Sidney explained,

"Gentlemen, we must now bide our time. Gordon Brown is hardly popular and there will certainly be a General Election in the not too far distant future. The man will probably hang on to power until the eleventh hour but that can still only take us to 2010. But we may have to wait much longer than that. In the meantime I would like to ask you gentlemen to gently sound out like-minded friends but without the slightest mention of the formation of a new party. We will need to form working-groups from among our number to meet regularly to formulate policy and we should all meet again in three months time to review matters."

And so was born the WDL, the Western Democratic League, and as far as the general population of the UK and indeed the entire western world knew, no such organisation existed.

CHAPTER THREE

ROBERT & ANGELA

Robert & Angela had been married in 1965. She was only nineteen years old and he was twenty four. Robert's father was a doctor and the boy was brought up in a large Victorian house in an inner suburb of Manchester. The house was also Roger's father's surgery and the only real contact the boy had with his working-class neighbours was when they came to Dr Pearson for medical attention. He was an only child and a lonely one. His mother did not consider the local children to be suitable playmates for her son and despite their best efforts, Robert's parents had failed to provide him with the companionship of a sibling.

Robert's mother was firmly of the view that the educational standards of the local schools were not appropriate to the son of a doctor and particularly one who was, she was certain, destined for a glowing future. He was therefore delivered each day to a preparatory school some five miles away where he was tutored and trained to enter and pass the Common Entrance Examination. This would enable him to continue his education at a famous public school in the south of England.

Robert's mother had been right about the educational potential of her son. He passed all his school examinations with flying colours and was eventually accepted at Oxford to read law. There, he gained a First and by the age of twenty two was articled to a prestigious firm of solicitors in the Deansgate area of Manchester.

At school Robert, as a timid young man, had avoided bullying by maintaining a low profile. This also resulted in him having no real social life and he had left school without a single close friend to his credit. He passed his time at university keeping very much to himself and when he started work he still had no real friends of either sex. He could and would chat amiably enough to his colleagues and members of staff but maintained his distance so that no one was ever aware of the real Robert Pearson lurking somewhere deep inside his psyche.

At the age of twenty two Robert was not only a virgin; he had never dated a girl. This did not seem to bother him one iota but his parents found his lack of social skills somewhat distressing.

"Robert," his mother would say. "You know our friends the Jamesons, don't you?"

"Yes of course I do Mother," Robert would reply, wearily.

"You know they have a gorgeous daughter called Sarah. Wouldn't you like to meet up with her one day?"

"Mother, I have met Sarah Jameson many times and yes, she is pretty but I am not interested. As I have told you before, I just want to further my career as a solicitor at the moment. Social diversions are of no interest to me."

And then he met Angela. She came from Wythenshawe and was hardly what his mother would have called 'top-drawer.' She was tall and slim with short blonde hair, an attractive figure and she spoke with a strong Manchester accent. She was one of

Robert's first clients at Nicholson, Hargreaves and Hyman and was consulting the solicitors regarding the possibility of obtaining an injunction against an ex-boyfriend who had been persistently stalking her.

After their first meeting, Robert found it impossible to think of anyone or anything else. Their backgrounds were worlds apart but somehow there was an attraction and the totally inexperienced Robert was overwhelmed by his feelings for the young woman. It must be said that Robert's infatuation with Angela had absolutely nothing to do with sex. In any case, all he knew of sex was what he had learned from his father who, as a doctor, was determined that his son should be well-acquainted with the 'facts of life.' It was of course the 'sixties' and the whole culture seemed to revolve round sex, music and drugs. Robert, however, to the relief of his mother, showed no interest in the 'disgusting goings-on' of the era.

Angela was due to see Robert again the following Thursday and he could hardly wait for the day to arrive. But arrive, it did and Angela was ushered into Robert's small office for her consultation. Robert then started to explain what legal remedies were open to her to persuade the man that if he continued making, what was fast becoming far more than a nuisance to her, he could well land up in jail. Robert quickly realised that the word 'nuisance' was definitely a misnomer and that Angela was becoming increasingly frightened by the man's behaviour. As the interview drew to a close Robert knew that he must find a way to see the young woman again.

"All this is naturally very upsetting for you," Robert ventured soothingly.

Angela nodded.

"Look, I cannot allow you any more time now but I would like to know more about you and how you came to be the object of this man's obsession," he said.

Again Angela nodded, this time allowing herself the luxury of a fleeting smile.

"I know you work in town," Robert continued, amazed at his own uncharacteristic forwardness, "would you like to meet me for a coffee at lunchtime one day?"

Angela had heard many chat-up and pick-up lines in her young life and was normally very wary when young men came on to her too strongly. However, she had taken a liking to the young solicitor. She had to admit he was good-looking and he had spoken to her at both interviews with obvious sincerity. The gentleness of his voice soothed her and it would have seemed bad manners she decided, to turn down a lunchtime coffee with her lawyer, particularly when he was such nice young man.

She smiled and accepted the invitation for the following day at noon, in the café of a well-known department store nearby.

The coffee meetings became an almost daily routine and then developed into regularly sharing a light lunch together. In the meantime the 'stalker' had given up pursuing her and had disappeared from the scene. So, the lunches became strictly social events and enabled the young pair to upgrade their acquaintanceship to real friendship.

Eventually Angela decided that in the absence of any such proposition from Robert that she would take the initiative and suggest an evening date. Robert was delighted as he had been trying to pluck up courage to ask her out for dinner for some weeks.

Of course Robert still lived at home with his parents and the sudden change in his routine from evenings-in with Mum and Dad to frequent absences quickly forced his mother to comment to his father.

"Robert has taken to going out quite frequently," she ventured.

"Yes," the good Doctor Pearson replied. "Probably got a girl friend and about time too! I was beginning to think he wasn't normal"

"I am sure you are right," his lady-wife replied. "So don't you think we had better find out who she is before it gets out of hand? She may not be suitable."

"The boy is twenty three years old and a qualified solicitor. Don't you think that he is old enough to know what he is doing? He seems much happier in his general demeanour and that is good enough for me!"

As the local doctor's wife in a poor working-class area she considered herself and her family only two steps down from royalty and one small step below the aristocracy. She expected to be treated like the wife of the local squire and in truth that was how most of the neighbours did treat her. There was no doubt that she was a snob who looked down on those of an inferior social order as little more than peasants.

"No," she said. "Sorry my dear, men, especially young men become entangled only too easily with women of the lower classes. If you won't talk to him, I will."

Due to Robert's work schedule and constant absences from the family dinner-table Mrs Pearson was obliged to wait until weekend to cross-examine her son about his social life. Breakfast on Saturday morning proved to be the perfect opportunity.

"Robert, my dear," she began.

"Yes mother," Robert replied.

"Robert, my dear, where do you get to these evenings? Your father and I hardly ever see you for dinner during the week."

"Mother," Robert lied, "I am very busy at work and often stay on in the office to keep my files up to date."

His mother nodded sympathetically.

"But my dear, you must eat," she commented.

"Yes of course I do," Robert replied allowing the display of a little impatience. "I eat dinner in town. Now that I am fully qualified I can at least manage to afford to feed myself, albeit modestly."

The determined Mrs Pearson had toyed with the interrogation long enough.

"I am sure you do not eat alone, night after night, so who are you dining with?"

"Oh, just a friend," Robert answered airily, now knowing exactly where the conversation was heading.

The doctor's wife now jumped in for the kill.

"A male friend or a female friend," she demanded.

Robert had a deep affection for his father and held his mother in awe. He had never before lied to either of them and in truth; he had never needed to consider this option.

"A female friend, if you must know," he replied, his face suddenly assuming a colour more in common with beetroot than human flesh.

"How long have you known this 'female friend'?" his mother demanded.

"Oh, about five or six months," Robert answered.

"Really, so long!" was the reply.

There then followed a torrent of questions for Robert to field. When she discovered from this interrogation that the young lady, Angela, lived in Wythenshawe, she gasped in horror. *There was only one thing for it,* she decided. *He had to bring her home to ascertain if she truly was a suitable lady friend for her beloved son.*

"I think you should invite her round for tea," she proposed. "I would like to meet her and so would your father."

As she heard herself saying these words, an inner voice was saying, *Wythenshawe! Wythenshawe! Are there any decent parts of such an area? What kind of woman has my poor boy become involved with? He is too innocent of the ways of the world; far too innocent.*

Robert, of course accepted the invitation on behalf of Angela who agreed reluctantly to the visit on the following Sunday afternoon. In fact Angela was curious to meet his parents, particularly in view of the warm tones in which he discussed his father and the obvious fear that his mother seemed to engender in her son.

The afternoon tea was a disaster although, all four present kept their feelings to themselves and indulged in as much polite conversation as they could muster. Angela had expected to take an instant dislike to Mrs Pearson after the way Robert had described her, although that was never his intention. Mrs Pearson equally had already taken a dislike to Angela from the moment the word *Wythenshawe* had been uttered by her son. *A common little tart*, she had decided, eyeing up the unfortunate girl who was dressed neatly and decorously as befitted the occasion.

Dr Pearson on the other hand, thought she was a nice sensible girl and although possibly not ideal material for a solicitor's wife, would certainly make a good companion for his previously lonely son. *I suppose the accent can be worked upon* he decided *if the relationship does develop into something more enduring.*

The two women both allowed themselves a sigh of relief when the young couple bade their farewells. As soon as they were out of earshot, the doctor's lady-wife turned to him and said,

"Oh my dear, How dreadful! This has to be stopped before it goes any further."

To which the good doctor replied,

"And how do you propose to do that? And for that matter, why?"

There then followed a fairly heated discussion which ended up with the lady of the house proclaiming,

"If you won't do something about this, I will!"

That evening, Mrs Pearson waited up for her son to return and made her feelings about Angela very clear.

"That girl is totally unsuitable for you. She will ruin your career and probably ruin your life. You must drop her at once."

Needless to say Robert did nothing of the kind and a week later Angela took Robert to meet her parents in their neat council house in the dreaded Wythenshawe. Her father was a council officer and her mother, a typist who also worked for the local authority. Robert took to them both immediately. They were warm, kind and friendly people. Their home, although by no means grand, was spotlessly clean, tastefully furnished and decorated and most important of all, was pervaded by an atmosphere of happiness and love.

That night Robert took Angela out for dinner and proposed that they marry as soon as possible. She accepted with alacrity and the wedding took place in the absence of Robert's mother, who never again spoke to her son. Dr Pearson, however, braved the wrath of his wife and attended the ceremony at the Registry Office in Bootle Street.

So began the married life of Robert and Angela Pearson.

CHAPTER FOUR

ACQUISITION & LOSS

The newly-weds purchased a comfortable semi-detached property in Didsbury. Neither of them had much by way of savings and their combined resources still required the addition of a small overdraft to make-up the amount needed for the deposit. However, both bank and building society considered that Robert, as a newly qualified solicitor, was an excellent risk.

For the first few months Angela was blissfully happy with her new husband. He was kind, considerate, helpful and even-tempered. In addition he was very house-proud and all their surplus cash, after living-expenses and mortgage payments went into transforming their home into what Angela's parents described as a 'little palace.'

However, all was not totally well in Angela's demi-paradise. There was one important area of their new life together that was causing her increasing concern. On their wedding-night Angela was not surprised to discover that her new husband, totally inexperienced in such matters, had great difficulty in consummating the marriage. On honeymoon, a week in Llandudno, he had shown little or no interest in the physical side of their relationship and this continued in their new life together. Sex occurred infrequently and always at Angela's instigation. Even then Robert found it difficult show any enthusiasm either emotionally or physically. Angela found this aspect of their relationship disappointing and not a little frustrating.

She was, however, of a taciturn nature and all else in their lives was absolutely ideal.

Incredibly, it took almost three years of an almost monastic existence before Angela raised with Robert the matter of a family of their own.

"Robert darling," she ventured one evening. "Now that you are a junior partner we do not really need my salary. Don't you think we could manage very comfortably without it?"

Robert agreed at once.

"Well then Robert," she continued, "wouldn't it be nice to consider starting a family."

Again Robert agreed but this time with a little less enthusiasm.

"We have a lovely life together and I am sure we could make a very happy home for a baby boy or girl of our very own."

Robert nodded. The idea of a child or even children quite appealed to him. The only problem was the means by which the child or children would be made. He loved Angela but literally hated having sex with her. He could not understand how anyone could enjoy the activity which by now seemed to be a major conversation point with most of his colleagues at the office whenever and wherever they socialised together. Not only that, but the television, movies and most of the population wherever he went seemed to be obsessed with the subject.

So battle commenced. Robert really wanted to 'make a baby' but making an erection was hard work and then ejaculating 'before the damn thing went down again' was a nightmare. The more they tried the harder (or rather the softer) it became. After a few months, all this fruitless effort was causing ripples in their relationship outside of the matrimonial bed. They started to snap at each other and gradually any attempts at sex ceased.

"Robert," Angela demanded. (There was no more 'Robert darling' now.)

"Do you want a family?"

"Yes," he replied quickly. "You know quite well that I do."

"Well how on earth are we to have children, if we don't have sex?"

Robert felt sad. They had been so happy together and this 'sex business' was ruining it. But he did want a child, *a son and heir or a daughter*, *whatever*, he thought.

"I think we should go and see the doctor," Angela suggested.

Robert was horrified. The idea of discussing such a delicate and private part of their lives with anyone else was anathema to him. Not only that; it was patently obviously that the fault was his, **not** Angela's.

"Look," he replied. "I think we should try again and hopefully we can make it work this time."

"Robert," Angela continued. "You do love me don't you?"

"You know I do," Robert answered quickly.

"Well then just try to relax and maybe we can do it this time."

Most normal highly sexed young men of twenty seven would have thrown themselves into such a project with great enthusiasm but not Robert. His attitude to sex had been scarred from an early age by the experience of having a domineering and prudish mother. Nor would he ever hear of discussing the matter with the doctor or with any other living soul and once again their endeavours did not bear fruit.

After a further six months the couple finally decided that if they wanted a child and Robert would not consider help from outside, they should adopt. An anxious period of interviews and more interviews commenced but a young solicitor in a nice suburb with a lovely young wife were ideal material and a few months later they were the proud parents of a lovely little boy who they called Jeremy.

When Jeremy was six years old Robert came face to face with his father. He was soon to retire from general practice and was building up a small network of other GPs who he knew would be pleased to welcome him as a locum.

It was 1975 and Robert had taken Jeremy into town to buy him a new coat at a large department store on Deansgate. Robert absolutely doted on the little fellow with his mass of black curly hair, large blue eyes and mischievous grin.

Dr Pearson had been attending a medical board at the Ministry of Pensions building nearby and decided to treat himself to a coffee before returning to his wife. Since Robert walked out of their life the older couple had become increasingly estranged. They blamed each other for the debacle that had destroyed their family and Mrs Pearson was virtually a recluse in the old house. She never smiled and rarely talked to her husband except on essential matters. The good doctor too was sad, if not broken-hearted, that his only son was virtually lost to him. However, he had his patients and his friends and even this tragedy could not force a normally happy man into the misery in which his wife now wallowed.

To reach the coffee shop Dr Pearson had to walk through the children's clothing department. As he strode along, anticipating a nice hot cup of coffee, he spied an unfamiliar but easily recognisable shape coming towards him holding the hand of a small boy.

The pair recognised each other simultaneously and the doctor was determined not to let the opportunity go by. He stopped in front of his son.

"Hello Robert," he said smiling. "And who is this young man?"

Robert had always adored his father and knew quite well that he was not responsible for their estrangement.

"Hello Dad," he replied. "How are you?" and then after a little justifiable hesitation he continued, "And how is Mother?"

"Oh, well enough," Dr Pearson answered in an off-hand way, "And who is this young man?"

"This is Jeremy," Robert replied and the little boy rewarded the older man with a dazzling smile.

"Look," the Doctor suggested, hiding his understandable distress that his son had never told him that he had a grandson. "How about having a coffee together?" He then fixed his gaze on Jeremy and continued, "and they have some very nice ice-cream here."

The meeting was a huge success and it was resolved and that the trio would meet again the following week.

Robert, of course told Angela about the unplanned reconciliation with his father but Mrs Pearson senior remained unaware that every Wednesday after attending his medical boards, her husband met up with their son Robert and grandson Jeremy for coffee and ice-cream. Indeed she had no idea that Jeremy existed and the bitterness of her attitude to life had denied her the one person who could have changed her outlook.

After the fourth meeting the Doctor expressed the wish to be re-acquainted with his daughter-in-law and it was arranged that she would accompany Robert and Jeremy to town the following week.

This meeting was gratifyingly successful and Dr Pearson returned to his cold and bitter wife happy in the knowledge that his son appeared to have a good marriage and that the little boy Jeremy who they had adopted was nothing short of a delight. He had been disappointed that the young couple had not produced a baby of their own and was a little shocked to discover that when he volunteered his professional help with the problem of procreation, he was quickly and unceremoniously told by his son that his assistance would not be welcome.

A routine developed over a few months of Angela collecting her son from school every Wednesday and then bringing him into town to the coffee shop where they were joined by Robert and his father. That was until one Wednesday late in November when, unusually the doctor had arrived first. *Probably delayed in the traffic,* he thought, *getting near Christmas.* But after waiting an hour he was convinced that something must have prevented them coming down to the city. Dr Pearson had the telephone number of Robert's office but by this time it was closed. He knew that Robert would never phone his home as his wife, Robert's mother might answer, and she was blissfully unaware of the regular family meetings.

At nine o'clock on the following morning, Dr Pearson lifted the phone on his desk in the surgery and telephoned Nicholson, Hargreaves and Hyman.

"Could I speak to Mr Pearson?" he enquired of the switchboard operator.

"Who is speaking please?" she enquired in a low voice.

"This is Dr Pearson, his father," he replied.

"Oh!" the young woman replied in a voice now scarcely above a whisper. "You had better hold on."

So the doctor held on, wondering at the strange reaction of the telephonist. And then another voice came on the phone. A strong male voice but also speaking in a strangely subdued manner.

"This is Julian Hyman," the man said. "Am I to understand that you are Robert's father?"

"Yes," replied the doctor, now seriously alarmed. "Is something wrong?"

"Very much so," Julian answered in a voice heavy with emotion. "I really hate having to tell you this but Robert and Angela were both killed outright last night in a motor accident on the M56."

The doctor was heartbroken. He had lost his son once through the attitude of his wife and now, just when bonds and contact had been re-established,

Robert had been snatched away again and this time permanently.

"Can I telephone you again later on to discuss arrangements?" he replied with tears streaming down his face.

He then realised that his late son's colleague, Julian, would find this a somewhat strange remark.

"We had been estranged," he continued by way of explanation. "It was only during these last few months that we had started to see each other again. Would you, by any chance have any contact details for Angela's parents?"

"Yes, we must have," Julian replied. "We have acted for them a couple of times. Just hold on and I will try and find the phone number and address."

Five minutes later Dr Pearson was speaking to his late daughter-in-law's father. He arranged to drive over to Wythenshawe that evening. It was the first time there had been contact since the marriage of their children six years ago.

Having told his receptionist of the terrible news and asked her to explain his absence to his patients, he drove home. How was he to tell his wife of the tragedy? And how was he to explain that unlike her, he had had the pleasure of becoming re-acquainted with their son over the last months and meeting his delightful little son who now looked upon him as a grandpa.

Once the news was broken, Mrs Pearson's cold hard façade crumbled and she broke into tears.

"What a waste!" she sobbed. "We may not have approved of his wife but at least we knew he was out there and pursuing his career."

"There is something else you should know," the doctor began tentatively. "We have a grandson, Jeremy, a delightful little six year old. Thankfully he was at home when the accident occurred."

This provoked another series of sobs.

"I did not even know she was pregnant," she eventually replied.

"She wasn't," the doctor answered. "They had a few problems in the bedroom department and decided to adopt."

"Oh!" his wife sniffed. "I wonder what the little boy is like."

"He is quite delightful," Dr Pearson replied.

"How do you know?" the heartbroken mother demanded, looking suspiciously at her husband.

"You may not like this but I have been seeing Robert, Angela and Jeremy every week for the last six months," he explained.

Then after a short pause to enable this information to be absorbed, he continued.

"I am going to see Angela's parents tonight; do you wish to accompany me?"

Mrs Pearson initially ignored this and commented,

"You have been seeing them for all this time and I never knew." Then after another sniff and a slow drying of her eyes with a handkerchief she continued,

"That is my own fault. It was my attitude that drove you to conceal this. Don't you think I have been longing to see Robert again? And now I never shall. That is my punishment."

"I want to meet this little boy. Jeremy, did you say?" Her husband nodded, astonished at the change in his wife's attitude. "I will come with you this evening and we need to discuss the little fellow's future with his other grandparents."

The doctor and a sad but transformed Mrs Pearson arrived that evening at the home of Angela's parents where they were soberly welcomed.

It transpired that their hosts that evening were both in poor health and when, to the astonishment of her husband, Mrs Pearson suggested that Jeremy should come and live with them, the suggestion was agreed to with alacrity, by all present.

And so the young Jeremy Pearson became a surrogate son for his tragically dead father and grew towards manhood. His home-life was totally different from that of Robert. The doctor had retired from general practice and although still busy in his medical career with work as an adviser to pension assessment boards, insurance examinations and other similar activity, he, his wife and grandson had moved to a small detached house in Bramhall, a leafy suburb of Stockport. Tragedy could have made Mrs Pearson even more bitter than hitherto but instead she mellowed and showed bountiful measures of love to her grandson that were so sadly denied to his father. He attended the local state school where he distinguished himself with excellent results and gained a place at Birmingham University where, in common with his late father, he elected to read law.

CHAPTER FIVE

JEREMY THE CHRISTIAN

His grandparents, in common with most of their generation had been fairly regular churchgoers. For their entire lives they regarded themselves as Christians. Their faith, however, was fairly superficial and it was at this involved but less than deeply religious level that they had raised their grandson Jeremy and his late father. It was, therefore, quite a surprise to the old doctor and his wife when Jeremy announced, when home from vacation that he had become interested in his religion to the extent of joining a Christian society at the university. When not studying the law, he was reading and applying his not inconsiderable intellect to analysing and learning in depth about his faith. The good doctor and his lady were now well into their eighties and waited until Jeremy was out of earshot before discussing this unexpected turn of events.

"I suppose it is a much better outlet for a young man than some of the shenanigans that go on at university," the doctor commented.

"Thank heaven he is safely away from the drink and drug culture that so many students embrace," his wife agreed.

"However, don't you think he is getting a bit intense about it all?" the doctor commented.

"Well, as long as it does not interfere with his studies, he could be involved in far worse things than Christianity," the old lady replied.

However, when Jeremy returned for the next vacation he informed them that he had arranged to spend Christmas at a retreat where he could undertake study and research into the origins of their faith. They gently tried to dissuade him and reminded him that this was a family time and they were deeply disappointed that he would not be with them to enjoy the usual festivities.

"Please forgive me," their grandson explained. "But this is wonderful opportunity to really understand the deeper meanings of Our Lord's teachings. And what better time than the season when he was born."

The old people had no choice but to accept and on the appropriate day Jeremy departed for the Seminary.

When the Easter vacation arrived he dutifully returned home. He did talk about his studies in the law faculty and these appeared to be progressing well. However most of his conversation was about the interest that seemed to be increasingly dominating his life, Christianity. Still he was home and he spent most of his time in the company of the old couple. Then the day before he was leaving to return to Birmingham he announced that he was spending the entire summer vacation in Israel visiting and learning about the birthplace of his religion. By now the grandparents were both very frail and had lived the last twenty years in total dedication to just one project - Jeremy. There was however, no dissuading him. He had already paid for his heavily subsidised trip out of part-time earnings at a bookshop in the Bull Ring and after a farewell phone call back to Bramhall, he caught the National Express bus to Heathrow in London for the El Al flight to Ben Gurion airport in Israel.

Most young men in their late teens or early twenties become infatuated with some delightful young woman but Jeremy was infatuated with a whole country. He had been welcomed at the airport by the Rev Thomas Gallagher who despite his Irish sounding surname was a Protestant and a member of a fairly fundamentalist group within the American Baptist Union. He took Jeremy to their headquarters in Jerusalem where simple but adequate accommodation was available for such students.

It was love at first sight for Jeremy; not I hasten to add with the good cleric but with the sights and sounds of the Holy Land. He adored Jerusalem and visited many its churches. He also derived great spiritual inspiration and comfort from visiting the Western Wall, the only remaining section of the Jewish Temple, where Jesus had prayed. During rest-periods from his theological studies he secretly and frequently took to walking over to the Wall. He was not sure what drew him there with such regularity. It began to worry him that he found so much more solace there than in the huge ornate churches that he had visited.

Over the next few weeks he was escorted by various members of the group to Tiberius where he imagined Jesus on the lake with the apostles. To Nazareth where Jesus had grown into manhood and arrangements were made for Jeremy to visit the

Church of the Nativity in Bethlehem, where Jesus was born.

It was on one of his clandestine trips to the Western Wall that he came face-to-face with John Rosenberg. He was also studying law at Birmingham and not only was he a Mancunian like Jeremy but he also supported Manchester City football club. In both cases these young men preferred City with their lower profile and detested the razzmatazz that surrounded the rival club Manchester United. Having said that, neither young man was a serious football fan. Their careers and fascination with their religions were the main features of their lives.

They had sat next to each other at lectures but in Birmingham that had been virtually their only point of contact. However, they quickly discovered over a coffee at the Old City Café that John's story was remarkably similar to that of Jeremy. Not only did they come from the same city and were studying law at the same university but they were both in Jerusalem to study and learn about their faiths; the difference was that John's faith was Judaism while Jeremy was a committed Christian.

It transpired that John's family had a small flat in nearby Talbieh and John asked Jeremy if he would like to visit on the Friday night to enjoy the meal and the ceremonies associated with the commencement of the Jewish Sabbath.

"I am sure you know that Jesus, who was after all a Jewish boy just like me, must have enjoyed his Friday night meals with friends and family the same way that we do," John explained.

He gave Jeremy the address and told him to arrive about seven o'clock in the evening.

"We might still be in Synagogue but my mother will be there and I can promise you a warm welcome from all my family."

Jeremy, who had been brought-up to be punctual, arrived on the stroke of seven and just five minutes after being admitted by his friend's mother, John, his father and older brother returned from prayers in a nearby synagogue.

"Ah, you are here already," John commented. "Have you been waiting long?"

"Not at all. I have certainly not been here for more than a few minutes and your mother has made me feel very welcome."

"Well, in that case may I wish you Shabbat Shalom? Do you know what that means?"

"Yes, of course," Jeremy replied. "That is how Jewish people wish each other a peaceful Sabbath."

John then introduced Jeremy to his father and brother. Arnold Rosenberg, the father was of medium height and build with iron-grey hair while the brother, Bernard, was a younger replica of his dad. John, on the other hand was sandy-haired with a far lighter complexion like the mother Rachel. They were all slim which, after the meal, nay banquet, they subsequently enjoyed, struck Jeremy as being surprising.

Looking round the table, during the evening, it occurred to Jeremy that he himself looked far more Jewish than John did.

This was Jeremy's first Friday night meal in a Jewish house and it was delicious. However, before a morsel was eaten Arnold explained that they had certain songs and ceremonies to usher in the Sabbath. Then Arnold blessed the wine in a goblet that vaguely reminded Jeremy of Holy Communion. However, John made a point of explaining that the prayers they said were to welcome Shabbat and had no connection with the Church ceremonies familiar to his friend.

Then with the wine blessed and drunk, they all trooped into the kitchen to wash their hands; accompanied again with blessings and a little ceremony. On return to the table Arnold said a blessing over two loaves of bread and cut one loaf up into slices for all to partake.

By this time Jeremy was really hungry and enjoyed every morsel of the meal from the chopped liver pate to the succulent roasted chicken and chocolate pudding desert.

These people really enjoy their religion, he thought to himself. *There is so much warmth. I suppose Christmas in a normal Christian family must be rather like this but that is only once a year.*

During the meal the Rosenbergs asked Jeremy about his own family and seemed genuinely sorry to hear about the loss of both of his parents at such a young age.

"You certainly have the most wonderful grandparents," Rachel said. "It must have been very hard for them bringing up a boy at their ages."

"Yes, they are very special," Jeremy agreed and began to feel guilty that he would not see them at all during the summer vacation.

"I believe you are also in Birmingham reading law," Arnold commented at the end of the evening. "I want you to know that you will always be welcome here and I hope you enjoy learning more about your faith while you are in Israel."

Jeremy thanked them profusely and with a little bow, wished them all Shabbat Shalom.

The Rev Thomas Gallagher expressed some interest when an enthusiastic Jeremy told him of the evening spent at the home of the Rosenbergs.

"That is very nice," he commented. "I am pleased that you have met someone who you knew from university. However, please remember you are here to learn about Christianity, not Judaism. The Jews love to point out that Jesus was one of them but how much, if any, of today's Judaism he would recognise, is very debateable."

Thomas Gallagher had in fact been born into an Irish family of lapsed Catholics and had become involved with The Baptist Movement while still at school in New Jersey. He was a passionate believer in the imminence of the 'Second coming' and followed the doctrine that for this to take place, the majority of the world's Jews must be settled in Israel. Then he believed Jesus would convert them all to the 'only true religion.'

Jeremy, however, found his faith shaken not reinforced by the pronouncements of his mentor. He was a highly intelligent young man and decided to return to Israel again, maybe at Christmas time but this time to learn more about Judaism.

CHAPTER SIX

TERRIBLE NEWS

Back in Birmingham Jeremy still felt very much in love with the land of Israel but now another contestant appeared, to try to win his heart. Jeremy had asked John; yes they were now close friends, to take him to a meeting of the Jewish society. Jeremy was just a tinge disappointed that the evening chosen was more about the struggle between Israel and the Arabs than religious Judaism but he enjoyed the cut and thrust of the debate that was the central piece of the evening's proceedings. And then he saw her. It must be said that Jeremy had seen this young lady in the distance, on campus, on a number of previous occasions. She was blonde and slim and seeing her now at a Jewish society function surprised him as, in his estimation, she did not look at all Jewish. She was however, talking to his new friend John which gave him the ideal excuse to approach.

Jeremy was confident but well-behaved where women were concerned. He did not share his late father's terror of the opposite sex. He had been in a couple of platonic relationships but they had not worked out mainly because he insisted on preaching to the young ladies about the desirability of remaining celibate until marriage. Jeremy was a very normal young man, unlike his late father. However, his religious training helped him to withstand the temptations that lovely young ladies offered to him.

"Hello John," he began, "and who is this pretty lady you are talking to?"

John had a girl-friend, Sophie Adler from Hendon in London *so what was he doing chatting away to this gorgeous creature?*

John welcomed him with a grin and said,

"This is Ruth Roberts from Leeds."

Jeremy treated Ruth to his best smile and asked her what she was studying.

After a short exchange of introductory information Ruth was more than a little surprised to discover that this talk dark young man, Jeremy, was not Jewish. However, he was charming and she decided that an invitation to meet for a cappuccino would be harmless and would certainly not be a step on the slippery slope towards intermarriage. Her parents were not particularly religious but it had been drummed into her from an early age that she was expected to marry within the faith.

They arranged to meet at a well known coffee bar on High Street and the couple appeared to have an instant rapport. By now Jeremy's interest in Judaism was growing apace and unlike maybe just a year ago, when he would have been keen to convert everyone he met to his brand of Christianity, he was only counting the days to when he would return to Israel to learn more about the Jewish way of life.

The young couple started to meet two or three times a week, these were not 'dates' it must be understood, just friendly meetings but John and Jeremy's other friends found that he had far less time for them. He took his law studies very seriously and was determined to gain a first-class honours degree. He had tended to lose interest in the Christian Society after his experience with the Rev Thomas Gallagher but he was avidly reading everything he could find on Judaism. He tried to learn from his new friend Ruth but quickly discovered that the level of her knowledge was only on a par with his grandparents' knowledge of the religion in which he was raised; peripheral. His other Jewish friend, John Rosenberg, was more knowledgeable and observant but Jeremy wanted to explore the Jewish way of life and belief system in far greater depth than even John could supply. He chatted with the Jewish campus chaplain, Rabbi Jack Abrams and he arranged Jeremy's next visit to Israel.

It was 23rd of November, a date that Jeremy would always remember when at six o'clock in the morning, he was awakened by banging on his bedroom door. It was one of the Indian students who had been about to telephone his parents in Mumbai from the bank of pay-phones in the hallway of the Hall of Residence.

"Are you Jeremy Pearson?" the young man shouted.

Jeremy jumped out of bed and flung open the door.

"Yes, that is me. What is the problem?"

"There is a phone call for you on phone number three. I was downstairs and heard it ringing. You had better come quick!"

Jeremy followed the Indian student downstairs and raced to the phone.

"Hello!" he said. "This is Jeremy Pearson speaking. Who is this?"

The voice on the other end was unrecognisable and appeared to be speaking between sobs.

"Please!" Jeremy repeated, "Who is this?"

"It is, sob! Sob! Grandma."

"Grandma, what on earth is wrong, you sound terrible?"

"It is Grandpa, I think he is, sob! sob! Dead," she managed to explain.

"Are you sure? Have you called the doctor? Are any of the neighbours with you?" Jeremy enquired, trying his best to keep calm.

"No," the old lady replied. "I just phoned you.

Half an hour later Jeremy was at New Street station awaiting the first train to Manchester out of Birmingham that Sunday morning. This was commonly known as the 'stopping train' and indeed to Jeremy it seemed to be more stopped than going and that at a painfully slow speed. It was 9.30am when the train pulled into Manchester Piccadilly and although his meagre funds hardly allowed for this extravagance he took a cab to the home he had shared through most of his childhood with his beloved grandparents.

As the taxi approached he could see an ambulance and a police-car outside the house. He paid the cabby and ran up the path into the house. A policeman was in the hallway.

"May I ask who you are?" the bobby enquired in a gruff but courteous manner.

"I am Jeremy Pearson the grandson. Is my grandfather dead?" he demanded.

The policeman nodded sadly and said,

"You had better come in here sir, I am afraid there is more bad news."

Once sitting in the lounge, Jeremy asked,

"What more bad news can there be?"

"It is your grandmother, sir. No doubt because of the agitated state she was in after finding her husband dead in bed, she tripped on her long nightgown at the top of the stairs, fell all the way down and died instantly, we think from a blow to the head. This is more than I should be telling you and full details will be given to you in due course.

"Are there any other relatives?" the bobby enquired.

"No, just the three of us. My parents died in a car crash when I was very young."

Jeremy had remained calm during all this exchange but now he broke down and wept. He wept for his grandfather who had passed on at a good age in his sleep, for his grandmother who had followed him just minutes or an hour or so later, for his parents who he barely remembered and for himself. He was alone, so alone, without a living relative to call his own.

Once the authorities had established, to their satisfaction, the rather obvious cause of death of the elderly couple, Jeremy, who had stayed on in Manchester, organised a joint funeral and the couple were laid to rest.

It was at the funeral that an elderly gentleman approached him.

"My name is Julian Hyman and I would like to offer my heartfelt condolences to you on the loss of your grandparents."

Jeremy nodded sadly.

"I realise they were going to die one day but to lose them both on the same day was such a blow. I do not know if you know that my parents died in a car crash when I was just five years old. My grandparents looked after me; they brought me up, loved me and saw to my education.

"Sorry, Mr Hyman," Jeremy continued. "My grandparents never mentioned you. What is your connection to the family?"

"I was your late father's senior partner in Nicholson, Hargreaves and Hyman. It was I who had the unenviable task of telling your grandfather the awful news after the crash. Since that time I have handled all Dr Pearson's legal affairs and I could do with seeing you before you return to Birmingham. It is Birmingham where you are studying, is it not?"

"Yes, that is right," Jeremy replied. ""Shall I phone your office to organise an appointment?"

"Yes please," Julian replied. "But tell my secretary that I said she must fit you in quickly, how ever tight my schedule may be." With that, he handed Jeremy a card and the two walked side-by-side to the double grave that had just been dug.

The Vicar spoke eloquently about the life of Dr and Mrs Pearson. He had obviously known them very well and Jeremy felt a deep sense of pride when he heard of all their achievements.

The following morning Jeremy telephoned Julian Hyman's office and spoke to his secretary.

"When would you like to come?" she enquired.

"As soon as possible as I need to return to my studies in Birmingham," was Jeremy's reply.

"Well, how about three thirty this afternoon. Mr Hyman has asked me to re-arrange his other afternoon appointments so that he can free for you," she explained.

Jeremy was grateful and expressed his thanks to Julian Hyman as soon as he arrived for their meeting. He had guessed that the solicitor wanted to see him about his grandparents' estates and, being more than aware that he was their only living relative, he was hardly surprised to hear that, apart from some charitable bequests, he was the sole beneficiary. He had been a virtually penniless student and now he was a young man of not inconsiderable substance.

"Will you wish to retain the house in Bramhall?" the solicitor asked.

"I would like to think about that," Jeremy replied.

"Other than that, all your grandfather's affairs were in very good order. Obtaining probate should be simple and straightforward. Would you like me to transfer a small sum to you now?" he continued.

Jeremy's first impulse was to say no. This was Grandpa's money and then he reminded himself that he could have no further use for it and he nodded sadly.

"Now Jeremy," the solicitor continued, "there is one other matter we need to discuss."

Once again Jeremy nodded.

"What is that?"

"It is about you, yourself," Julian explained.

"What about me?" Jeremy retorted, feeling suddenly a little uncomfortable.

"This is extremely difficult even for me," Julian ventured.

"Look! There is no easy way of asking this question. Do you know that you were adopted?"

Jeremy felt a shiver going down his spine.

"Adopted? What do you mean adopted? I know my grandparents adopted me when my parents were killed but that is not what you mean, is it?"

The solicitor shook his head.

"Your parents never managed to have a child of their own. As you know, this can happen for a variety of reasons. They therefore decided to adopt a baby and you are that baby."

Jeremy broke out in a cold sweat and reached for a tissue to mop his brow.

"So my parents weren't my real parents and my grandparents likewise?"

"Look Jeremy," Julian said reassuringly. "None of them could have loved you more than the way they did, if they had been your birth parents."

"So, who are my real parents and why didn't they want me?" Jeremy replied after a pause.

"We have no idea who they were. Your mother died in childbirth and we do not even have information about who she was, let alone your father. Your grandfather tried and tried to discover who they were and gave up in the end.

"We have one tiny piece of evidence, a worthless trinket that you could buy on any cheap jewellery stall," Julian explained.

"Here it is." He unwrapped a tiny tissue-paper parcel that had been lying on his desk. Inside was a metal charm of the sort that young girls like to hang on a bracelet. It was in the shape of a seven branch candelabra.

"It is valueless but is the only link we have to your birth-mother. Please take it. It is your property.

However, please remember that to all intents and purposes your family were the Pearsons. You are Jeremy Pearson and you have been given a wonderful start in life by your grandparents. I know this news has been a terrible shock. I suggest you return to Birmingham as soon as you can and immerse yourself in your studies. That is what your grandfather would have wanted for you."

Jeremy rose and gravely shook the hand of the solicitor.

"You have been incredibly kind and I am sure I will soon learn to accept the news you have given me today."

Then Jeremy bethought himself to ask the solicitor a question.

"Would you mind if I asked you a personal question?" He enquired.

Julian Hyman looked at the young man oddly. He realised he was a sincere decent person but what could he possibly want with him of a personal nature.

"I suppose so," he ventured uncertainly. "But I can't promise to reply until I know the nature of the subject.

"It is nothing to cause you any discomfort," Jeremy replied. "I just wondered if you were Jewish."

Julian was somewhat taken aback by the question and although not particularly religious he was proud to consider himself as such.

"Yes, I am," he replied, "but why do you ask?"

"I am thinking seriously of converting. I was brought up as a Christian but have found that the more I investigate and learn about Judaism, the more I feel it is the religion for me."

"You do realise that we are probably the most persecuted people on the face of the earth. Are you sure that you know what you are going into?" the solicitor answered. "I cannot pretend to keep all the laws or even many of them but for a convert there is a huge amount to learn and to convince the Rabbis that you would keep them all."

"As I said," Jeremy answered, "I am thinking seriously about this and I thought you must be Jewish, so hence the question. I hope I have not offended you in any way. You have been most kind to me."

"Not at all," Julian replied, his wrinkled face breaking in to a broad grin. "However, if you want my advice I would finish your law studies in Birmingham before deciding your future."

This latter exchange had occurred while both Julian and his young client were standing. The solicitor now shook hands again with Jeremy and wished him great success in his future life. Jeremy pocketed the tiny charm after rewrapping it in the tissue paper and bade his grateful farewells to the solicitor.

Chapter Seven

Jerusalem - Christmas 1990

Jeremy was heart-broken. He had loved the old people dearly and now they were gone. He was also shattered by the news of the mystery surrounding his own origins but he knew he must get on with his life. On return to Birmingham he went to see the Jewish chaplain Rabbi Jack Abrams. He told him, of course, of the double tragedy he had just endured and asked him if he felt it was still right to visit Israel over the Christmas holidays, now only three weeks away.

"I cannot tell you what to do. Even if you were Jewish it would be hard to direct you. It must be how you, yourself feel. Whatever I was to advise, and whatever you ultimately decide may turn out to be the right or the wrong decision. I am sorry but it must be you alone who decides.

"On the one hand the trip could be therapeutic," he continued, "but only if you do not allow yourself to be immersed in feelings of guilt. I gather you were a wonderful grandson, so you should have nothing reproach yourself for."

"Well Rabbi," Jeremy answered, "if I do decide to go can I still count on your help and advice in the final planning?"

"Of course you can," the Rabbi replied grinning.

Apart from feeling guilty that he was off to Israel so soon after the death of his grandparents, Jeremy also felt that he was being disloyal to his own Christian tradition. How could he let the words of one fanatic, the Rev Thomas Gallagher, drive him away from his upbringing in the protestant church. He pondered hard and long on this but his desire to know more about Judaism just grew and grew.

When all is said and done, he decided, *how can it be wrong to learn about the religion that Jesus himself followed?*

He was equally determined not to ask the advice of any of his friends. After his conversation with the Rabbi he knew it was for he alone to decide.

Needless to say, some two weeks later Jeremy was off to Israel armed with a list of places to visit and people to talk to, supplied by Rabbi Jack. He had now become a relatively wealthy young man. His grandparents had lived comfortably but hardly enjoyed an extravagant lifestyle and as a General Practitioner Dr Pearson had always earned a healthy income. Then there was the house in Bramhall. In the early 1990s this was a popular middle-class area and the property would sell quickly at a good price. He therefore decided to put it on the market and after a short telephone call to Julian Hyman, an estate agent was instructed.

The trip to Israel was a huge success and ended with Jeremy promising a new friend, Rabbi Shlomo Kahn, that he would return in the summer. This was his last year in Birmingham and once he graduated he had decided to take a year out to continue his studies into the faith that so intrigued and fascinated him. However, he still regarded himself as a Christian but one searching for truths that had so far escaped him in the religion of his family.

Back in Birmingham he started to attend meetings of the Jewish society on a regular basis and his friendship with John Rosenberg blossomed. He also started to date Ruth, despite her feelings of guilt for becoming the girlfriend of a non-Jewish boy. However, the relationship cooled very rapidly when Jeremy realised her lack of commitment to Judaism. Although he was the non-Jewish boy in question, he realised that he could not approve of a Jewish girl who was prepared to date him knowing him to be a Christian boy. She was a very attractive girl but he quickly discovered that their interests on all subjects, including religion were poles apart and the short romance came to a speedy conclusion.

The summer marked the end of his course in Birmingham. Jeremy had achieved his ambition of gaining first class honours. Oh, how proud his grandparents would have been, he pondered, with tears in his eyes. He met all his friends for a celebratory drink in a pub that was popular with the student fraternity and with promises to stay in touch, all the graduates made ready to start the next phases of their lives and careers.

With the degree he now had, he knew that, if he was to practice as a lawyer, he must choose between the bar or a career as a solicitor. But that was not the only decision on which he agonised. If the truth be known, he felt that his whole life was now at a crossroad. The kind of lawyer he was to become, a barrister or a solicitor, worried him little. What caused Jeremy sleepless nights was whether to have a future as a Christian or as a convert to Judaism. Again he returned to Israel and by the time he alighted from the bus that had ferried him from the airport, the decision was made and he started a course of study that lasted two years and ended with his conversion to Judaism. This was not without serious misgivings when he considered the fact that all this was only possible as a result of his grandparents leaving him in a financially independent state. *What would they have thought of me converting to be a Jew?* He pondered. But unsurprisingly there was never an answer to this question.

During his two year stay in Israel he looked forwarded to the occasional visits from England of his friend John Rosenberg. John had been astonished to learn of Jeremy's decision to convert and at first had tried to dissuade him. He suspected that his friend had decided to embrace Judaism while still in a highly emotional state as the result of the sudden loss of both of his grandparents. Little by little John came to realise that taking the path of conversion had been well thought out and that his friend was determined to see it through to the end. Although John was fairly religious and came from a family background steeped in Jewish practice, his friend Jeremy displayed an ever increasing thirst for knowledge and commitment well beyond John's personal capacity.

Now once again, Jeremy stood at the crossroads. He had been converted. He was a religious Jew and wore the badges of his new faith with great pride. He had grown a beard; he wore a black velvet skullcap and his Tsitsit (fringes) hung down over his trouser waistband on both sides of his hips. He had taken the Hebrew name Yirmiyahu and had been called to the reading of the Torah in synagogue by this new name. He had achieved both of his previous ambitions and was now a Jew with a first class honours degree in law from an English university. He had lived frugally in Jerusalem while undertaking his conversion course and his capital remained virtually intact. Now he needed another challenge and what was that to be?

CHAPTER EIGHT

BESSIE AND GERALD CHARLESTON (1969)

They had been 'trying for a baby' as the expression went, for four years now. With more than a little embarrassment and temerity they had eventually visited their GP, Dr Stuart Robinson. They had then separately undergone numerous tests which only served to increase their determination when they were both given a clean bill of sexual health.

"Maybe you are trying too hard," the doctor suggested. "Just relax and I am sure it will all be fine."

But still nothing happened. In fact the situation was worsening as however much they tried to heed the advice of the doctor, the tension was having an effect on the health of them both. Bessie, always of a nervous disposition, had lost her appetite and Gerald was lying awake night after night wondering what was wrong with him when his erections could just vanish at the crucial moment.

It was then that Bessie took to drink. She had always enjoyed a glass of mild beer of the local brew and now, completely out of character, she had taken to secretly calling in a pub near her work for a couple of pints before returning home. Then one evening, feeling particularly depressed by their problem, she had consumed chasers in the form of two double measures of gin, which meant dipping into the housekeeping money. She had returned home noticeably drunk and feeling guilty for squandering their hard earned cash in such a way. Bessie could hardly be described as a seductress but when, Gerald arrived home from the bank he was quickly aware of her condition and astonished by the way she was now attired, in a dressing-gown and nothing else. To be attacked by his drunken wife in this condition somehow excited him and this time there was no erectile dysfunction.

When she sobered up later in the evening Gerald felt obliged to discuss with her the dangers of alcoholism; his father had been over-fond of a 'drop' for years before ending up in an early grave. Reminding her of this had the required effect and for the next few weeks she abstained from the 'demon drink.' Then she missed her period and told Gerald that she suspected that she might have conceived. A visit to Doctor Robinson confirmed that she was pregnant and he proceeded to instruct her on how to conduct herself while carrying the baby.

Later that year Bessie was delivered, by Caesarean section, of a premature baby boy. Gerald's mother had re-married and now lived with her new husband, a teetotaller, in the north of Scotland and both of Bessie's parents had died young. Neither of them had been blessed with siblings and growing up as 'loners' had convinced them that they had no use for friends or family (had there been any!) They casually told their respective work colleagues of the arrival of little Sidney and Bessie despatched a letter to Inverness, to her mother, to tell her she was now a grandmother. They both waited anxiously for the day when their young son could home. However, this was not to be and the poor mite died in the incubator that had been his only home while on this earth. Quite understandably the couple were broken hearted. They returned home to Islington in a state of utter dejection.

Just three weeks later they were surprised by a ring on the front-door bell. They were not used to visitors, other than the milkman and the window-cleaner who both arrived for their money no later than six o'clock. By this time it was nine o'clock so who could this be, calling at such an unearthly hour?

Gerald opened the front-door to find their doctor on the step.

"Hello doctor," he said quietly with his eyes downcast. "Won't you come inside?"

"Would you like a cup of tea?" Bessie enquired as soon as he was seated.

"No thank you," the doctor replied. "Look, you must know why I have come. I am dreadfully sorry to hear about your poor little baby boy. He did not really have a chance. He was so premature that many of his internal organs had not yet developed. You tried for so long and so hard to have a baby and it seems so cruel that he has been snatched away from you."

The doctor turned to Bessie.

"I hate to mention this but I have a very good reason for doing so. I assume you have told Gerald that bringing this baby into the world has left you unable to conceive again."

Bessie nodded thinking the doctor seemed determined to make matters even worse by mentioning this additional overwhelmingly painful fact.

"I know it is early days but if ever there was a couple who deserve to have a child it is you two," the doctor continued. "Dare I ask, so soon after your loss; would you consider adopting a child?"

It was earlier that day when one of his partners in the practice had told Doctor Robinson that a lovely healthy little boy was now in council care and did he, by any chance, know of a suitable home for the baby. The doctor quickly telephoned and told the authorities that he knew just the ideal parents for the little fellow.

The doctor surveyed the faces of this rather lacklustre couple who, after their terrible experience, would undoubtedly love and cherish an adopted child. Maybe this could be the making of them both, he thought.

Gerald looked at Bessie and they both exchanged fleeting little smiles as they nodded in unison.

Bizarrely, the couple had told neither her mother nor their work colleagues of the death of their own baby. Even in such tragic circumstances they could not share their grief; they had both been alone all their lives, and only looked for comfort and solace from each other.

The new baby arrived and was quickly christened in a private ceremony at the local church. He was given the same name, Sidney, after the tiny mite who had not survived. He was a strong, vigorous, happy baby and he helped to heal his parents broken hearts until the memory of that poor little soul was buried as deeply in the minds of his parents as his tiny body lay buried in a neglected corner of the churchyard.

They decided that Sidney must never know that he was adopted and as time went by; both Bessie and

Gerald came to almost forget that Sidney was not their natural born son.

CHAPTER NINE

YOUNG SIDNEY

Sidney shone at nursery school where he was universally adored by the staff and by all his little friends. He shone at primary school and although his teachers found him a pleasure to teach and made him a class favourite, this did nothing to diminish his popularity with the other children. From a very early age he had developed instinctively the ability to make almost everyone that he met, like him. This continued into secondary school and at university he was much in demand as a speaker at debates which usually culminated with him being on the winning side. He had a number of relationships with girls and although, for varying reasons, these were not of significant duration, he always remained on good terms with his 'ex's. There was, however, another side to Sidney; one that was only initially seen by his mother and father.

At the tender age of six Sidney was already proving to be a demanding child at home. This did not mean that he demanded 'things' like new toys but rather he demanded his parents complete obedience; a case of role-reversal on a grand scale. His parents had been so happy to have him that, right from the start, they had given in to his every whim. At school, for his own reasons, he behaved impeccably but at home he would expect to be waited on 'hand and foot.' From four years old he had refused to address his parents as Mummy and Daddy and told them this was childish. He called them Mum and Dad and, call them frequently, he did.

"Mum, could you please switch on the TV," or "Dad, can you fix my bike?" or "Mum, I will have some more pudding?"

He sensed the docility of both Bessie and Gerald and ruled them with consummate ease. Being people of very average intelligence, they took all this in their stride and little realised how totally spoilt their son was. Sidney was delighted when Bessie gave up her work at the solicitor's office as this meant that she would be even more at his beck and call. A lad with other kinds of demands could have gone completely off the rails but Sidney was only interested in having power over other people and by one means or another he managed this.

As he grew into manhood the Charlestons were deeply proud of their son's scholastic achievements and when he graduated from Cambridge with a first, their joy knew no bounds. He invited them to attend the graduation ceremony and did have the good grace to introduce them to his bride-to-be and her parents, although he had never previously intimated that he had a girl-friend and wished to marry.

They were completely out of their depth with the Craigwell-Smyths and breathed a collective sigh of relief once the wedding was over.

"I can't say that I feel very comfortable with Sidney's new in-laws," Bessie confided to her husband.

"They seem rather snobby to me," Gerald replied. "Well, as long as the boy is happy, that's what counts. I hope we don't need to see too much of them."

Of course, not only did they not see the senior Charlestons but apart from a very occasional phone-call from their son for birthdays and Christmas, he had quietly removed himself from their lives. Their docility, however, knew no bounds and they accepted the situation with fortitude.

"Sidney is building a wonderful career in the army," Gerald would remind Bessie. "He is grown-up now and must make his own way in the world."

As time went by the Charlestons began to see their son's face on the television and what ever secret disappointments they might have harboured as a result of Sidney's failure to keep in touch, they knew now that he was a famous man and could hardly be expected to have time for his aging parents. Neighbours, who knew who Sidney was, now approached them and tried to develop friendships with the couple. From knowing no one in the street they were now greeted by most of the local people who would whisper, once the Chalestons were out of earshot,

"Do you know who their son is? He is that Colonel Charleston who is always being interviewed on telly."

It was shortly after Sidney's latest stint in Iraq that Bessie began to suffer with severe bouts of pain in her stomach. This coincided with nausea and weight-loss and Gerald had to persuade her to visit the doctor's surgery. Amazingly, she found herself face-to-face with a now elderly Doctor Stuart Robinson. Bessie had assumed that he must have long-since retired and on her rare visits to the surgery previously, she had never seen him.

"Well, hello, Bessie isn't it?" the doctor enquired. A considerable feat of memory after some thirty five years. "How are you and Gerald keeping?"

"He is fine," Bessie replied. "But I am not feeling too well."

She proceeded to tell him of her symptoms and the doctor arranged for blood-tests at the local hospital.

As she rose to take her leave the doctor said,

"How is your son? He must be in his mid-thirties by now."

"Oh, "she answered, "he is fine. He is in the army. Have you never seen him on telly? He is a colonel now; Colonel Sidney Charleston."

The doctor was astonished. What on earth could this somewhat arrogant but highly intelligent man have to do with this humble little old lady?

"Well I had no idea that the little baby you adopted would become so famous."

Bessie suddenly panicked. They had never told Sidney that he was adopted. Indeed, both she and Gerald had almost forgotten this fact.

"Doctor," she said, looking extremely embarrassed, "he does not know that he is not ours from birth."

The doctor looked at her in amazement.

"What possessed you to do that?" he enquired, horrified.

"He always seemed as if he was our own poor little Sidney who died in hospital. We know we should have told him but never got around to it," she explained lamely.

The doctor looked down at his desk as if reading a document but the desk was completely clear.

I must not let this failure to tell their son the truth about his origin cloud my judgement. I may have found them the baby all those years ago but that does not make their concealment my business. Indeed, I must say I do not much care for the fellow anyway; strikes me as being as hard as nails. I think this poor woman is very ill and why should I give her any additional worry.

At last the doctor spoke.

"The important thing is to get on with your tests. Please take the note to the hospital without delay and we will see what other investigation is needed when the results come back."

Sadly Bessie was suffering from an inoperable cancer of the abdomen and had secondary growths in various other vital organs. Within three months she was dead and a lonely broken-hearted Gerald was arranging her funeral in the same churchyard where their tiny baby son lay.

The Colonel managed to take time off from his other duties to attend the funeral. A number of their neighbours attended, ostensibly to pay their respects to a woman they hardly knew, but really in the hope of seeing the man, fast becoming a television celebrity, in the flesh.

She was buried in a grave next to the tiny headstone that marked the grave of the first Sidney. Gerald had not given, even a thought about what would happen if Colonel Sidney saw the engraving and it was only as they turned from Bessie's grave, after the internment, that his son, his adopted son, saw the inscription.

"Whose grave is this?" he demanded of the old man.

Although Gerald was of fairly limited intelligence, he realised immediately that their subterfuge was about to be discovered. He tried a lie,

"That is the grave of your little brother," he answered quaking.

Sidney looked down at the grave again and said,

"It can't be. This baby was born in the same week as me, in the same year and he has my name."

Gerald realised that the secret he and Bessie had kept for so many years could no longer be sustained.

"Come back and have a cup of tea and I will tell you all about," he said nervously.

Needless to say Sidney was furious. He cared not one iota for the feelings of the father who had cared for him during his formative years. The fact that Gerald was mourning a wife and Sidney should have been mourning a mother, had no relevance to him. He had been, he decided, fed a pack of lies for all these years and now he had just one task to undertake, to find his real parents.

This proved to be too much for even the indomitable Colonel Charleston. The identity of the poor woman who had given birth to him had never been discovered and if she had known the name of the father of the child, she had taken that information to the grave with her.

"There is only one item that I have kept all these years and that I believe belonged to your real mother,"

Gerald enquired nervously. "Shall I go upstairs and fetch it?"

"Yes, of course, get it," the Colonel barked, "and hurry up. I am due at a meeting in an hour."

The item turned out to be a cheap metal charm of the type young girls attach to a bracelet. It was in the shape of a seven branch candelabrum.

"I don't know what use this piece of rubbish can be," he grunted. "Anyway I'll take it but it looks pretty useless to me."

He persuaded his father to tell him who had arranged his adoption and he went to visit Doctor Stuart Robinson. He had taken, unusually for him, an instant dislike to the young army officer. However, even if he wanted to, there was little he could add to what Sidney already knew; and that was virtually nothing.

The place of birth was stated as 'Brixton' which Sidney was in no hurry to divulge to his wife, his in-laws or to anyone in his circle of friends, admirers and associates. The local registrar was unable to add to this information.

"I am sorry, Colonel, this is quite irregular but for some reason 'Brixton' is the only address we have."

Sidney's knowledge of Brixton was fairly scanty. He knew that in 1969 when he was born, the area had a large population of immigrants, mainly from the West Indies. He had a number of Brixton born soldiers in his regiment and they were excellent men and a credit to the British army. He swore to himself that their colour was of no relevance and that he was not, nor ever could be a racist. However, he did begin to study himself in the mirror for any signs of excessively curly hair and darker skin tone. Like many members of the UK population he was, in fact, fairly dark skinned but in the manner of other south Europeans; Spaniards, Greeks and Italians. No matter how hard he studied himself, he could find no evidence of Afro-Caribbean blood.

Eventually, the matter of his origin had to be put aside and he knew he must concentrate on his career as an army officer and politician. These were to be the stepping stones to a far, far greater prize, he reminded himself.

Chapter ten

A Trip to Manchester

By the time Jeremy stepped off the plane from Israel, for the first time as a fully-fledged member of the Jewish people, he knew what he must do. His law degree would stand him in good stead in his future life but the law he wished to practice now was the Law of Moses in all its beauty and complexity. He no longer had a permanent abode in England with the disposal of his grandparents' home in Bramhall. He checked into a hotel in Birmingham, his last city of residence, albeit as a student in the UK. As soon as he had put away his few possessions, he tried to telephone the Birmingham Jewish Student Chaplain, Rabbi Jack Abrams. However, he was no longer in post having been offered a position with a synagogue in Manchester, the previous year. Jeremy had spent all of his childhood and schooldays in the area and it somehow pleased him that the man, who had given him so much good advice, was now resident there. It was therefore quite easy to track down the Rabbi who had set him off on the journey that was to end with him becoming a convert to Judaism.

He lifted the telephone in the hotel bedroom, having realised, that at the prices they charged for local calls, he must go out as soon as possible to purchase a British mobile-phone.

A pleasant sounding female voice answered,

"Hello, this is the Altrincham Synagogue, how can I help you?"

"Could I please speak to Rabbi Jack Abrams?" Jeremy enquired.

"Who is this speaking?" the lady responded.

"My name is Jeremy Pearson and I knew the Rabbi when he was student chaplain in Birmingham."

"I am sorry, Jeremy," the lady replied. "He is out at the moment but should be back very soon for a meeting with a Barmitzvah boy and his parents. If he gets back in time I will ask him to call you before the meeting," she explained, "but it may well be later on when he phones. Is it something I can help you with?"

"No, no! It is the Rabbi I need to speak to. I am currently staying in a hotel in Birmingham. Please ask him to phone me on 0121 987 6543, room number 412."

"Certainly Jeremy," the lady replied. "I will tell him as soon as I can catch up with him."

Jeremy sat on the hotel bed contemplating the phone and wondering where he was going to get a kosher meal in this city, so familiar to him in the days before he had religious dietary requirements.

He picked up a book and started to read and then the phone rang.

"Hello Jeremy, what are you doing in Birmingham? The last I heard you were in Jerusalem."

"Rabbi," Jeremy replied warmly. "Thank you for calling me back so quickly. I need to see you as soon as possible. Could you squeeze me in tomorrow?"

"How would tomorrow morning at say 11am suit? It would be here at the synagogue. Do you know the address of the Altrincham shul?"

Years ago when Jeremy lived in Manchester he was more interested in the location of churches than synagogues but the Rabbi soon told him how to find his way there from the Metrolink station.

"Just one other thing," Jeremy added hastily. "Do you know where I could get a kosher meal as there do not seem to be any Jewish restaurants here?"

The rabbi gulped in surprise. Many young people decided to convert and then fell at the first hurdle. Obviously Jeremy was not in this category.

"Just sit tight in your room and within the next half hour you will receive a phone-call. Just remind me where you are staying tonight and I will see you tomorrow!"

Unbeknown to Jeremy most major British hotels had arrangements to obtain and supply very adequate pre-packed kosher meals and he was delighted when he received a phone-call to discuss what was on offer that night.

He enjoyed the dinner and spent the rest of the evening reading. By 10 o'clock he was fast asleep and woke at 6am just at the right time to say his morning prayers. He then packed his few belongings, paid the hotel bill and walked briskly to New Street station to catch the train to Manchester Piccadilly.

Chapter eleven

Altrincham

Jeremy arrived at the Altrincham Metrolink station at 10.45 and was outside the synagogue just ten minutes later. He was admitted by a pleasant middle aged lady who told him her name was Janice and that the Rabbi had been called away.

"He is really sorry but the matter was urgent and we had no way of reaching you. Do you want to give me a mobile number now, while we remember?"

"I have only just returned to England after studying in Israel for the last four years," Jeremy explained. "I have not yet had time to buy a mobile but I will get one later on today and phone you through with the number for the Rabbi."

"Fine," Janice replied. "Do you want to wait for Rabbi Abrams to return or come back in an hour or so?"

"I will tell you what I will do while I am waiting," Jeremy answered with a smile. "I will go into town and buy a mobile and be back here by 12 o'clock."

The shops were only a short walk away but Jeremy found that without a permanent place of abode in the UK he could only buy a 'pay-as-you-go' machine but that was more than enough to make him 'contactable.'

He strolled back to the synagogue and arrived just as the Rabbi returned.

"Jeremy, I am so sorry," the Rabbi apologised, "but it was an emergency. Anyway, here I am now and what can I do for you?"

They were now in the Rabbi's rather cramped office and he gestured to Jeremy to pull up a chair.

"I assume you do realise that I am now fully converted?"

"Yes, that looks rather obvious from your clothing but I will need to know all about your conversion; the names of the Rabbis and which Beth Din (ecclesiastical court.)

By the time Jeremy had finished telling Rabbi Abrams all these details and shown him supporting documentation, he could see he was impressed, particularly with the names of some of the most respected figures in Judaism.

Rabbi Abrams sat back in his chair.

"So, Yirmiyahu ben Avraham," he said, using Jeremy's new Hebrew name. "How can I help you? You seem to have done very well on your own, so far."

Now it was Jeremy's turn to sit back in his chair.

"I want to become a Rabbi."

Jack Abrams let his jaw fall open as he surveyed the young man sitting opposite him.

"I assume this is a well-considered decision. Did you discuss it with your Rabbis in Israel?"

"No," Jeremy replied with engaging honesty. "It had been in my mind for most of the time I was in Israel but the final decision was only made on the plane bringing me back here."

"I see," answered the Rabbi thoughtfully. "Are you sure this is not some spur of moment fancy that will pass?"

"It took great determination to convert and now I am Jewish, I am not supposed to be treated any differently from any other Jewish boy wanting to dedicate his life to his people," Jeremy replied, looking somewhat crestfallen. This was not the reaction he had expected.

The Rabbi sat forward again feeling slightly awkward in that he had just been corrected.

"You are absolutely right. Throughout the ages we have been blessed with converts who became great Rabbis. I am sure you will know of the origin of the celebrated Rabbi Akiva for example?"

Jeremy nodded,

"Yes of course."

"Tell me Jeremy, just one thing puzzles me. Why come back to England? In Jerusalem there are Yeshivot (theological colleges) on almost every street corner."

"Long before my mind was finally made up," he explained, "I considered that option and then I became certain. I am English; I talk like an Englishman and I had learned much about Anglo-Jewry from John Rosenberg and my many other Jewish friends. I think this is where I can do the most good, so here I am."

The Rabbi glanced at his watch. He had a Shabbat sermon to prepare.

"Can you come back tomorrow morning at 10 o'clock? We need to discuss all this in much greater detail. Have you somewhere to stay in Manchester?"

Jeremy smiled. His smiles always lightened the darkest day.

"I will see you tomorrow as arranged and thank you for devoting so much time to me."

He liked Altrincham and checked himself into a small inexpensive hotel in the town. There were two other Synagogues in the area and Jeremy took a bus to where he had been told he could buy a Kosher take-away for the evening. This was near one of the other synagogues and he quickly discovered what time they would be saying the afternoon and evening services. The caretaker let him in and he spent the rest of the afternoon studying in their library.

At their meeting the following day, Rabbi Abrams was able to advise Jeremy how to set about achieving his ambition. He supplied Jeremy with a list of theological colleges that would be appropriate for him. He then offered to personally approach the Rosh Yeshiva (college head) of one such institution in Gateshead, north-eastern England which he felt would be ideal. The gentleman in question was out when Rabbi Abrams phoned but later that day Jeremy received a text message on his new mobile telling him to contact this college head who would be interested in granting him an interview. The interview took place the following day and Jeremy so impressed the Rosh Yeshiva that he left the meeting with an offer of a place.

So Jeremy Pearson started another long journey, this time to become ordained as a Rabbi. However, he did not travel all the way on his own as eighteen months into his studies he was introduced to Miriam Goldfine (also a theological student at a nearby seminary) and in 1996 they were married. Her father was the Rosh Yeshiva (head) at another college in Gateshead, where the ceremony took place, and the young couple stayed on there after their wedding to continue their studies.

Chapter twelve

Unexpected Visitors (2004)

Rabbi Jeremy Pearson had been a diligent and enthusiastic student at the college in Gateshead. He had the ability to absorb vast amounts of knowledge on the entire myriad of subjects that encompassed Judaism. His previous life as a gentile law-student also stood him in good stead when he was appointed minister of a small community, Southpool, on the Lancashire coast. He had the advantage over most young Rabbis of having seen the world from two distinctive vantage points, first as a Christian and then as a Jew.

The finances of the synagogue which served just two hundred souls were sorely stretched but Jeremy looked upon this poorly paid stipend as wonderful experience in the real world and away from his recent cloistered existence in Jewish academia. He wanted to serve his community and serve, he did! His work also brought him into contact with the other ministers of religion from the majority Christian faith. The two principal ones were Father Joseph O'Riordan of the largest Roman Catholic church and the Reverend Tom Smallwood of the main Church of England establishment. It was Rabbi Jeremy who proposed that an inter-faith group of churches, the synagogue, the mosque and the Hindu temple be organised. His colleagues were equally enthusiastic as it gave them an opportunity to approach the local town council and other similar bodies and to speak with one voice on issues of faith and morality. It was no small compliment to Jeremy, still years junior to the others that the other faith leaders insisted on him becoming chairman of their group.

The population of the town was just 53,784 and for most of them life was good. There was fairly full employment and although everyone knew of the dangers of terrorism from fanatical Islamists and the destructive power they had released on New York, the attack on London had not yet happened and most British people, especially in the smaller towns, went about their business with confidence in their personal security. As for the economy, Gordon Brown as Chancellor and Tony Blair as Prime Minister had been telling them for years how lucky they were to live in such a wealthy country and they believed it.

The most troubling aspects of life at that time revolved around a minority of young people whose drink and drug culture made many of the streets of Southpool difficult to navigate for those of more senior years. It was this subject that most exercised the minds and meetings of minds of the All Faith Group at their now monthly meetings. It was resolved that this should be the subject of their sermons on a particular week in July although Jeremy pointed out that preaching to the converted would achieve little or nothing. Meetings were then arranged with the police and with the Town Council and as result a public meeting was called. Rabbi Jeremy was the youngest member of the faith group but somehow he found himself as the chairman that evening and his words were received with great enthusiasm by the local people. Suddenly they felt that they now had a champion in their midst and very quickly he became a local hero. The council of the Synagogue was somewhat taken aback by the almost tsunami-like wave of popularity for their new rabbi.

"We are very pleased with the way you have settled down here," the President told him. "We can hardly complain if your work for the wider community has made you so popular but, with respect, you just need to be careful that all this public work does not cause you to neglect your duties here."

The young Rabbi naturally assured the President that his first priority was the Synagogue and gently pointed out that, if Jews were ever to be a genuine 'light unto the nations' they must reach out to all, Jews and Gentiles alike.

Within two years Jeremy had been approached by one of the larger synagogues in Manchester and the Southpool Hebrew Congregation knew that they must release him to continue his good work elsewhere.

His new congregation had invited him to join them knowing full well that he was something of a media star and that he would be constantly in the eye of the wider public as a result of frequent television and radio appearances. If the truth be known they were more than happy to bask in his reflected glory and the membership of synagogue began to increase rapidly which more than justified his appointment.

Apart from having had a previous incarnation as a Christian, Jeremy also had one other huge advantage over most young Rabbis. He was very comfortably off and this gave him the confidence to speak out sternly to his community on religious matters and to take an independent line with the Synagogue council when they saw fit to complain that his outside activities might cause him to neglect his duties to them. Eventually he suggested that they should reduce his salary and employ another even younger Rabbi, fresh out of seminary, on a part-time basis to ensure the congregation received the necessary level of spiritual guidance.

Jeremy and Miriam were now the proud parents of four handsome little boys and with all his communal and public activity he made it a rule to devote time to their upbringing. He never forgot that he had been denied the love and guidance of his parents at such a tender age although he was ever mindful of the way that his grandparents had tried to fill this gaping hole in his young life.

It was a rather murky evening in late November, some eighteen months after Jeremy and Miriam had arrived in Manchester during the early evening time that Jeremy always described as his 'family time' when the doorbell announced the arrival of an unexpected visitor. The Rabbi was just enjoying reading a children's bible story about the baby Moses to his two older children and Miriam went to answer the door. Outside were two smartly dressed men.

"I know this is a terrible imposition just dropping in on you like this, but may we speak to the Rabbi?" the older man began.

"I must tell you that if there is one time almost as sacred as his praying time, it is the time he likes to spend with his children," Miriam explained. "In any case, can you tell me who you are and maybe make an appointment during the day when, I am sure, my husband will be pleased to see you?"

"I really am sorry to descend on you in this way. We have just had a meeting and Edward Kornfeld and I are due to return to London this evening. Incidentally my name is Jack Rothberg."

"Can you at least give me some idea of what you need to see my husband about," Miriam replied.

"All I can tell you is that it is to protect the future of our country that we wish to see the Rabbi," Rothberg replied somewhat melodramatically.

Jeremy had heard the conversation and decided the time had come to rescue his wife. He handed the book to his older son Yitzy and promised to return in a few minutes. He stepped out into the hall and made his way to the front door.

"I am Rabbi Pearson," he said. "Do you have a serious problem that requires my urgent help?"

The Rabbi had a neat but full beard but there was something about him that made Jack Rothberg stare. The Rabbi on the other hand felt uncomfortable at the scrutiny.

"Look gentlemen. I only see people at this time if it is an emergency. Is your request because of an emergency?" he enquired.

"No," Kornfeld replied, noting that his colleague seemed to have been struck dumb. "We were in Manchester for a meeting, as Jack explained to your wife and we could do with a chat about a matter of public concern."

"Is this matter of public concern an emergency?" the Rabbi enquired. He was well accustomed to handling men of all classes in many situations and prided himself on his patience in difficult circumstances. These two men however seemed to be far too insistent given their own admittance that the matter was not especially urgent.

It was then that Rothberg decided to re-enter the conversation. He was still staring hard at the Rabbi in a most disconcerting way.

"Have we met before?" he demanded somewhat abruptly.

"I am sure we have not," Jeremy replied. "You say you are from London and I know relatively few people there. I suppose that now you are here" he continued with resignation, "and so insistent, I could spare you ten or fifteen minutes. Please come in."

He invited them into the dining-room and enquired if they preferred tea or coffee? He then excused himself to ask Miriam to prepare the drinks. As soon as he left the room Jack Rothberg whispered to his companion,

"Does he remind you of anyone? He is the absolute double of Sidney Charleston."

"Yes," Edward Kornberg replied. "I suppose he does have a passing resemblance but how you can tell with the thick beard covering his face, beats me?"

At that moment the Rabbi returned carrying a tray containing three cups of hot coffee. He was beginning to feel a little ungracious at the way he had resisted inviting the men into his house. Hospitality to all comers is important in Judaism and Jeremy began to feel his lack of a warm welcome was well below the standard he normally required of himself. He knew that had they been poorer members of the Jewish community looking for help, financial or otherwise, they would have been invited into his home at once. Somehow, the Savile Row suits had made him feel less friendly towards them – a form of inverted snobbery he decided.

"Now gentlemen," he began, with a smile. "How may I help you?"

"I am Jacob Rothberg, the chairman of the Jewish Council for Democracy, and this is my colleague Edward Kornfeld. We know from your media pronouncements of your concerns for the future well-being of the United Kingdom and all its peoples." Rothberg spoke as if he was addressing a public meeting but after the disastrous start to the men's visit, Jeremy was determined to remain patient and friendly. "We would like to offer you full membership of our group."

"I have to admit that I have only heard very vaguely of your organisation. It is true that apart from looking after my congregation, I do take an active interest in public matters affecting the whole population. However, I am not interested in party politics as such, however commendable the aims."

The two men looked somewhat crestfallen. They had been told that the Rabbi would be an ideal member of the JCD and eventually of the WDL, although that was a matter for the future. The executive of the JCD had decided that to have a Rabbi 'on-board' would be a tremendous achievement and it now seemed that their errand had been unsuccessful.

"We would really be honoured if you would at least consider joining us," Kornfeld added. "May we leave you some information about our aims and objects."

"Gentlemen," the Rabbi replied. "I thank you for thinking of me and I will certainly read through your prospectus but it would not be appropriate for me to join any organisation with even a remotely political agenda. "

Jeremy made to rise when Jacob Rothberg suddenly enquired,

"Do you know Colonel Sidney Charleston?"

"No, not personally," the Rabbi replied, "but who in this country has not heard of him and read his interviews and pronouncements in the newspapers?"

"Rabbi," Rothberg continued, "do you know that you bear a striking resemblance to him?"

"Really!" Jeremy answered. "I don't watch television so I have only the vaguest idea what he looks like from press photographs and yes, I suppose there is a vague similarity. Anyway gentlemen, thank you for coming."

It would soon be time to return to Synagogue for the evening service and within a few days, the interview was banished to the inner recesses of his mind where it would lie until events some years hence would give him cause to recall it.

CHAPTER THIRTEEN

ELECTION AND DEJECTION

At the inaugural meeting of the WDL in 2007, Sidney had informed his friends and colleagues that he was certain that Gordon Brown and his Labour Party would lose a General Election and Sidney waited impatiently for this election to be called. It was obvious to all that Prime Minister Brown knew just as well as Sidney that he was staring into the jaws of defeat. He, for the best or worst, of personal reasons, was determined to hold on until the eleventh hour, namely Thursday 6th May 2010, before launching himself into what he knew would be virtual political oblivion.

In the four years since the unofficial inception of the WDL, his colleagues had been busy spreading the word to all like minded people but on the basis that this was just a loose association, not a political party and that their job would be to support the Conservative party and particularly those on the right fringes. The result of the poll, however, was a deep disappointment to Sidney and his ever expanding group. The Tories could only form a government with the support of the Liberal-Democrats. They and their policies, on almost every issue, were total anathema to the WDL and its supporters.

Sidney was a patient man. He knew that timing was absolutely essential if his grandiose plans were to succeed. However, he found it quite depressing to watch the steady flow of what he considered 'socialist' legislation emanating from a government whose prime-minister was supposed to be a Conservative.

Some of the 'cuts' in spending that were necessary after years of a spendthrift Labour government were vital in those difficult times but far, far too much money was being wasted on the pet projects of the Liberal party. So the time had come to act.

It was four years since the original group of fifteen had met together to listen to Sidney and now, once again, this same gathering of influential people was invited to Sidney's house. On this occasion however, each of the men had his own group of fifteen under his own direction and each participating member of that group had another group under him and so on. This meant that there was now a total of 759,375 people in the United Kingdom who were loosely affiliated to Sidney's organisation without being aware of it. As far as all of these people, excepting the original group knew, they had simply been invited to join a current affairs debating group on the internet and to answer questions on matters in the news. Each group member selected his own members and should any of them betray, through answers to the questionnaires, a lack of sympathy with the aims of the organisation, they were replaced. This was a simple process as they had their email addresses deleted from the next month's questions. There was only one other rule and that was for each member to ensure that his own group was up to the required strength of fifteen.

As soon as all fifteen men were seated Sidney asked Rupert, his man-servant, to take orders for tea or coffee. Once this was supplied, the meeting started.

"Gentlemen, It is hard to believe that four years have elapsed since our last discussions took place here, in this very room. During that time I have had many meetings with you all, on a one to one basis, but now the time has come for us to act as a group. Gordon Brown and his Labour party have gone, as I forecast, and they now have a new leader. He is further to the left than Brown and much more dangerous. Sadly, the electorate of the United Kingdom let us down and we finished up with a hung-parliament that resulted in this dreadful coalition. Our potential members may not realise this but we should already be three quarters of a million strong, as a result of the groups of fifteen, and the time has come to act.

"Our first task," he continued, "will be to make the WDL into a bona-fide political party. This is a simple straight forward process and within a month from now you should receive an email confirming that registration of the party has been formalised. Then you will be requested to pass the good news all the way down the line and ask all our on-line friends to complete an application form and email it to us with a first year's subscription of £10."

At this point, Sanjiv Joshi of the Hindu Defence League raised his hand to speak.

"Yes, Sanjiv," Sidney invited. "You have something of relevance to what I have just said that you would like to add?"

"Yes, Sidney," Sanjiv replied. "Forgive me interrupting at this stage but I wondered how sure we can be of the co-operation of the members of the groups of fifteen in joining the new party?"

"You are absolutely right to raise this point and I was just about to comment on this myself," Sidney responded with a look of mild irritation on his face that was somewhat at variance with his soothing words. "The quality of our potential membership will only be as good as you people, and how good your ability was to choose and motivate those below you in the chain. If we can start with a membership of just half a million that will still be more than adequate. Remember, now we are about to come out into the open as a political party we should start to attract serious media attention and that should attract many more right thinking people to our ranks."

After some further discussion the meeting broke up and the attendees returned to their homes, businesses and families to await the promised email.

On Monday the first of November 2011, Justine Fletcher, Sidney's PA, pressed the 'send' button on her computer to shoot off the application form for membership of the WDL to the original fifteen founder members and onwards to some three quarters of a million British citizens. Justine an attractive willowy brunette was a twenty-five year old Oxford graduate, the daughter of a good friend of Sidney's, Colonel Timothy Fletcher. Little could she have imagined the impact, the simple and routine action of sending this email, would have on her life and those of countless millions?

Chapter Fourteen

The Cabinet Maker - 2014

By February of the New Year, Sidney knew for certain that his project was a resounding success. The never-ending problems in the Euro-zone, the crumbling economy of the USA under its distinctively left of centre government and the failure of the UK Coalition government to speak with one voice had catapulted millions of British people into desperately pledging allegiance to the new party. All of the right-wing press had welcomed the WDL. The more populist journals had gone completely overboard in their praise for Sidney, the acknowledged leader and his group of primary activists. The fact that they, between them, represented almost every major ethnic and national group in the UK was proof that at last the population of the UK was speaking with one voice and this was of course, the voice of Colonel Sidney Charleston. There was naturally some dissention and faint sounds of disquiet were already being voiced by the Guardian, the BBC and other media organisation with a left facing agenda.

Sidney was being interviewed daily on television. With the world economy in such dire straits every new piece of bad news resulted in the Colonel being asked for his views on why it had occurred and what needed to be done to rectify the situation. Only Sidney and the WDL, so it seemed to most of the population, had all the answers. Foreign governments began to sit up and take notice.

Then the long-predicted collapse of the Euro-Zone occurred and many of the nations that had joined in the single currency could no longer pay for the goods that they had hitherto imported from the UK. The ensuing chaos resulted in hyper-inflation and most imported foodstuffs soon became unaffordable to the majority of the population. Unemployment quickly rocketed beyond the six million mark. There were demonstrations and riots in the streets but this time the demonstrators were decent hard-working British men and women suddenly unable to provide for their families. No one was now looting fashion and electronics stores. That all seemed so long ago but in reality was just four years previously. The British Prime Minister realised that his government had lost control of the situation and he resigned. The coalition had originally promised in 2010 to serve for a full five year term and this was only a few months away. He knew the government had failed in almost every aspect of running the country. A general election was called and the WDL was swept to power in a landslide poll. As the leader of the party the Queen invited Sidney Charleston to form a government. He had been waiting for this day for many years and most of the major cabinet appointments were initially from his original group of fifteen. These were the people who Sidney knew he could initially rely upon. Jacob Rothberg was invited to be Chancellor of the Exchequer. His experience in the fields of banking and economics should be invaluable in view of the disastrous state of the public purse. Ahmed Yamani became First Secretary of State for Foreign and Commonwealth Affairs. If anyone could deal with the

Jihadists and Islamists in any attempt to take control of the Western World, he was the man. Angus Ferguson, a tough uncompromising and narrow-minded Scot, became Secretary of State for Home Affairs. He would have the unenviable job of calming and policing the understandably agitated population. John Pilkington became Secretary of State for Justice. He was a lawyer with a fine reputation. Jane Jackson was to be Secretary of State for Health. Sidney had chosen a number of other ladies to be in his first cabinet. They were, of course women of power and influence in their own fields. All the men and women chosen by Sidney were known for their absolute loyalty to him and for their background of unscrupulous conduct when confronted with insoluble problems. From the group of fifteen there was only one notable absentee; the Hindu, Sanjiv Joshi. Sidney had regarded Sanjiv as a friend and knew his commitment to the cause was without doubt but he was also something of a pessimist by nature and this was no time for negative thinking. Instead he appointed another Hindu and a loyal member of the WDL to a Ministerial post.

The Colonel appeared on the Television and personally announced his choices for government posts to a nation anticipating little less than miracles from their new Prime Minister.

That evening Sidney Charleston sat in his study. He had fought long and hard, had been incredibly patient and now he had won the prize of a lifetime; he was the Prime Minister. However, what kind of a prize was this? The country, along with most of the western world was in a long deep recession. The people had elected him to be their saviour but how could he achieve this in a world in turmoil? He had harnessed the ocean waves and was about to inherit a tsunami. He knew that the power he now had could quickly become the equivalent of a poison chalice. However, Sidney's first instinct throughout his entire life was using whatever position he had to benefit just one person, Sidney Charleston. He resolved to stay in power, come what may. He would use whoever and whatever was required to achieve this end. He had been elected on the basis of being a democrat. But democracy for Sidney was just a means to an end. He was only too well-aware that the Nazis in nineteen thirty-three Germany had gained power through the ballot-box. He had now done the same. However, he was not a racist and the entire population would serve him as virtual slave-labourers not just certain targeted groups, as Hitler had done. Once the honeymoon with the people was over, and he knew that it could not last more than a very few months, he resolved to take all necessary steps to retain power indefinitely.

Chapter fifteen

Trepidation

Rabbi Jeremy had now been the Rabbi at the large Synagogue in Manchester for a number of years. During this time he watched with horror the slowly deteriorating economic situation, not only in the UK, but throughout the western world.

He had originally started to take an interest in the moral decline of the young people in Southpool and this had made him focus not only on his own small community but on the wider population. He could hardly miss the effects of promiscuity and although the majority of his middle-class Jewish congregation still married and then started families, there was an increasing number of his congregant's children setting up home with members of the opposite sex without going through any kind of marriage ceremony, let alone a Jewish one. Naturally and as a direct result, there was a steadily increasing number of babies born outside wedlock.

He had also been obliged to deal with the horrific problems arising from drug addiction. By the time of the General Election in May 2010 he knew that his own group of ministers of religion were virtually impotent to deal with the fast growing range of social difficulties and to bring some sanity back into the lives of the people.

Jeremy had watched with deep concern the growing number of Members of Parliament who were accused and then admitted to what was tantamount to fraud. *What chance do the young people have to lead decent honest lives if this is how their leaders behave,* he agonised. *What an example!*

Then there was the underlying and ever-present threat of Islamist violence. His good friend the Imam Yusuf Khalil discussed the problem with him privately on a number of occasions. Yusuf preached tolerance and respect in his Mosque but was very aware that there were fanatical young Muslims in his own community who laughed at him and called him a traitor to the Prophet Mohammed and the Holy Koran.

Finally, in the two years leading up to the 2010 election there had been a serious world banking crisis and everywhere in the countries described as western democracies the financial situation was in desperate trouble.

The Rabbi could hardly have failed to hear about the WDL and its leader Colonel Sidney Charleston. Much of what he said resonated well with Jeremy. When Charleston preached about morality, honesty, respect and clean living, of course these words coincided completely with his own world view. Why then did he feel uncomfortable about the huge wave of popularity for this new political party and its leader? Jeremy avidly read everything that appeared in the newspapers on the state of the country and indeed the entire developed world. As an important religious leader he was interviewed regularly on how the faith communities viewed the fast deteriorating economic and social scene. He told his followers that they must reconsider what their priorities were. Jeremy felt that gross materialism was largely responsible for the present plight. Sadly these words fell on deaf ears. The people did not want to hear about managing with their old possessions. They felt that their peer groups only judged them on what they had and not on who they were. Gradually his voice was silenced. Invitations to speak for the faith groups on radio and television and interviews with the newspapers became a thing of the past. All the people cared about was returning to the 'good old days.' His synagogue viewed this as a mixed blessing. Certainly he was now devoting himself entirely to them and when the Assistant Rabbi left he was not replaced. This was also a vital financial decision as their accounts were suffering from the increasing number of their members now unemployed and unable to contribute to the congregation's funds.

In the midst of all the turmoil Jeremy was invited to a meeting with the Synagogue executive where he was given the choice of leaving or accepting a huge cut in his salary. This was at a time when the income from his inherited capital was bearing very small returns but Jeremy felt that as long as he could feed and clothe his family, he must accept whatever he was offered. Miriam, his wife had taken a teaching post at a local school and this helped to just keep their heads above water.

And then in 2014 came the resignation of the coalition government followed by the overwhelming victory of the WDL. Rabbi Jeremy hoped and prayed that a new, united, strong government would improve the lot of the people but he had misgivings. Everything he read about Sidney Charleston worried him. He was still saying all the right things but Jeremy was convinced that the remedies the WDL had to offer were too trite, and too plausible. They were being swallowed by a desperate and gullible population and Jeremy fervently prayed that he was wrong.

CHAPTER SIXTEEN

FROM BAD TO WORSE

It could not be denied that the new government set about their tasks with determination. However, very few of them had even the remotest idea how to run a country. The Prime Minister Sidney Charleston and the Chancellor of the Exchequer Jacob Rothberg were exceptions as they had been preparing for many years, for the day when they would be voted into power. However, even Jacob Rothberg was never aware of the insatiable lust for power, for its own sake, that his old friend Sidney Charleston kept well concealed, even from him.

In the aftermath of the election, calm returned to the streets of British cities. The entire population breathed a sigh of relief and sat back expectantly, waiting for a steady and significant improvement in the economic situation of the country. However, the new WDL government soon discovered that the trite theories of its leader were no answer to the total collapse of the Euro and the isolationism of the new American government. The USA had its own similar problems to deal with and the answer of their new right-wing Republican administration was to cut themselves off from their old friends and allies in Europe.

In the UK unemployment continued to increase at an ever-expanding rate. Food prices rocketed and stores selling consumer goods in all sectors closed their doors. Within six months of the election the high streets of Britain were fast becoming no-go areas. The banks, which just a few years ago had triggered the original world-wide collapse of national economies, began to close down, one after another.

Again demonstrations and riots on the streets were a daily occurrence and the new Home Secretary rushed a bill through parliament giving extra powers to the police and providing for a huge increase in temporary prison accommodation.

The newspapers and other media were now demanding to know what the new government was doing to alleviate the chaotic situation. The answer of the administration was to proclaim a state of emergency.

It took only another three weeks before the police, now armed, opened fire on demonstrators and the death toll began to rise steadily.

Naturally enough the media blamed Sidney Charleston whose response was to order the arrest of editors and journalists who had the impertinence to criticise him and his government. Even the Royal family was warned that the government would brook no interference from them and realising that this WDL government was completely unscrupulous, the young princes waited quietly in the wings to see if and when they could make any kind of contribution to improve the lot of the people.

The vast majority of decent, sensible people viewed with horror, the descent of the United Kingdom into a dictatorship. But to whom could they turn? The previous government, a coalition, had inherited a serious economic situation from their predecessors in the Labour Party and now the promises of Sidney Charleston had proven to be worthless. The situation had gone from bad to worse; far, far worse.

"We have to take complete control," was the oft expressed mantra of the new Prime Minister. "Anyone, and I mean anyone, who tries to make trouble and undermine our government will have to be arrested and detained under the special powers act."

There were only some seventy members of parliament who were not members of the WDL after the election. These comprised forty five Conservatives, twenty two Labour and five Liberal-Democrats. However all three party leaders were among those elected and in the early days of the WDL government they banded together to make an attempt to be some kind of an opposition. The Conservative leader, as leader of the second largest party, was chosen to be the leader of the opposition and he set about questioning Sidney Charleston and his cabinet about the steps they were taking to put Britain back on track. The WDL had little or no interest in giving serious thought to these questions. They had over four hundred MPs and they could afford to completely ignore the demands of the Opposition. Eventually the government abolished Parliamentary Question Time and the cabinet suspended all meetings with the tiny and toothless Opposition. Then a further act of Parliament suspended the whole democratic institution 'until the economy recovered.'

The only forum now open to the three party leaders was through the media and journalists eagerly sought out the three gentlemen for comments on the fast deteriorating economic and social situation within the UK. Sadly, these journalists and political commentators failed to recognise the fact that they were simply sentencing themselves and the opposition politicians they interviewed, to indefinite spells of what the WDL described as 'preventative detention.'

"If the members of the opposition parties cannot refrain from attacking our country, they must be silenced. We cannot tolerate what is tantamount to treason," Colonel Sidney Charleston thundered.

The police were deeply unhappy with the work they were now called upon to undertake. A secret meeting of Chief Constables was called by the Commissioner of the Metropolitan Police, Sir James Hobein, to take place in Nottingham. There it was resolved that the Chief Constables of Manchester, Leeds and Birmingham be authorised to request an urgent meeting with the Home Secretary, Angus Ferguson, to voice their serious concerns. Amazingly, it took three weeks to arrange, due to his 'busy schedule.'

The meeting eventually took place at the Home Office and had just begun when an additional and unexpected attendee appeared. The Prime Minister knew exactly what would be the policemen's complaints and he was determined to only allow them to make them in HIS good time. He was not about to be held to account by a bunch of senior cops.

As soon as he was seated alongside Angus Ferguson, he spoke.

"I hope the Home Secretary will forgive my unscheduled attendance this morning, but I have great respect for our police and the way they carry out their duties. If there are matters that the government needs to know about, regarding law and order, I, as Prime Minister would like hear them directly from you gentlemen."

The Home Secretary said, "Of course, Sir," in such a way that made it crystal clear that he knew the Prime Minister would arrive to take the meeting.

The Chief Constable of Manchester, Sir James Robertson, spoke first.

"Sir," he began, "I must tell you that we, as the representatives of all the Police forces of the United Kingdom, are delighted to have the opportunity to speak directly with the Prime Minister."

"I have to enquire," the Prime Minister replied, "on whose authority you claim to speak for all the police forces of the country?"

"Sir," Sir James replied."I came hear to discuss a wide range of policing matters with the Home Secretary after an informal meeting of Chief Constables last month. However, as most of the matters are a direct result of the policy of your government, I will be pleased to enumerate them for you."

Sidney Charleston replied with barely concealed anger.

"You come hear after an informal meeting and expect to be treated seriously?"

"Yes Sir, we do," the Chief Constable of Manchester replied. "However, our meeting was with the Home Secretary. We did not know that you would be attending the meeting but now you are here, are you going to hear us out?"

"Before we go any further," the PM replied angrily. "You are all the Chief Constables of large and important cities but surely, if what you have to say is so important where is the Police Chief of our most important and largest city, London?"

"As I just stated Sir, we had no idea we would be meeting you. Had we had that information I know my good friend Sir James Hobein, the Commissioner of the Metropolitan Police would have accompanied us.

"Well Sir, are we or are we not to now proceed with the substance of our concerns?"

Sidney was furious. *How dare these men come here to voice 'concerns,' as they call it. They are servants of the government and paid to uphold the law and public order.*

"No you may not," the PM replied. "If you really need a meeting to voice these 'concerns' as you call them, whatever they are, may I suggest you request one officially through your own body, The Association of Chief Police Officers."

"But Sir," James Robertson said, "is this meeting to proceed or not?"

"The answer to that question is an emphatic No!" Sidney replied, now thoroughly annoyed. "Go away and come back when you speak officially for your colleagues and bring James Hobein with you."

Had the PM not been entirely confident in the inability of the police chiefs to speak with one voice, he might have handled the short meeting with more tact. However, he had a number of friends and indeed party members among the Chief Constables and other senior ranks. He knew Nottingham, Liverpool and Glasgow would back him to carry on with the policy of silencing dissent and as soon as the meeting finished he arranged a phone conference. It was these three police chiefs who had alerted him to the informal meeting and had supplied a full report of the proceedings.

It only took another two or three days for the three policemen who had visited the Home Office on that fateful day, to be arrested on charges of 'corruption.' They were quickly replaced by men who had shown unswerving loyalty to the Prime Minister.

Sidney then arranged, through his friends, a large scale dismissal on the grounds of cost, of all members of every police force in the UK whose loyalty to Sidney and the WDA was in any way suspect. The only 'honest cops' who remained were those who realised the necessity to lie low. Those who spoke out were partially replaced by untrained men and women, often with a history of violence who could be relied upon to terrorise the dissidents among the population.

Next Sidney turned his attention to the army. Many of the senior officers were personal friends and he explained to them that as a result of wide-spread corruption in the police, soldiers would have to be drafted in to help to subdue the population, now becoming increasingly agitated.

Britain was fast-becoming a police state and with most of the remaining police and the army firmly loyal to the Prime Minister, the unhappy population knew not where to turn.

CHAPTER SEVENTEEN

AN INVITATION TO HAVE A FUTURE

Rabbi Jeremy Pearson had stopped giving sermons on any current matter some years ago. He still spoke most weeks in the Synagogue but his topics were kept carefully to the lessons to be learned from the weekly readings of the Torah. Even here he was extremely careful as anything that smacked, ever so slightly, of containing a political message had to be avoided. This was if he was to avoid the fate of a number of his faith colleagues who had allowed a political message to creep into their sermons. The Archbishops of Canterbury and York had both been replaced with men loyal to Sidney. The Chief Rabbi had left the country some years ago, ostensibly to visit Israel, and had not returned. All preachers, be they Christian, Jewish, Muslim, Hindu or other persuasion, knew that they must not criticise the government or make any overtly political statements, if they were to retain their jobs. There still were a few brave souls who tried to ignore the new rules and they finished up in prison to await trial on a variety of trumped up charges.

The people however were returning to religion in droves. They hoped that in God's holy places they would find comfort for their miserable lives but the men of faith who were God's representatives were in fear of their own lives. They knew that if they stepped out of line their voices would be completely silenced and they watched and waited.

Such a one, who watched and waited, was Rabbi Jeremy Pearson. He had been political before the WDL came to power but in a non-party manner. He had worked hard, in co-operation with other men-of-the-cloth to improve the lives of the people but now he knew he must retain a very low profile. He had seen dictatorships abroad in more primitive societies but he never imagined in his wildest dreams that this could ever happen in one of the greatest democracies the world had ever known, the UK. And it had all happened so fast.

Manchester now had a Mayor, a loyal WDL man named Thomas Appleby and he ran the city much as he wished. He drove around in a late model Rolls-Royce, the cost of which would have fed many starving families for a year. Like the cabinet ministers in London, all the big city bosses were protected by large numbers of armed police outriders. The new Chief Constable who had replaced the unfortunate Sir James Robertson, after the fatal 'accident' that had befallen him while under arrest, was a man of doubtful character and had been due to be investigated on corruption charges. Like many other senior politicians and functionaries, his commitment to the new regime was easily bought with a large salary.

So far, the government had steered clear of taking any steps that would have hurt the royal family. They, recognising the dangers, had all moved into Buckingham Palace where the Queen, a frail old lady still lived and grieved over the terrible plight of her people. At least they were all together. However, they were virtually prisoners in the palace, but it was a prison without guards or locks. Prince Charles and his two sons had watched in horror as the realm he had expected to rule, was overcome by tyranny.

All over the UK resistance was stirring but such was the hold that Sidney Charleston and his men had on the country, most of these disorganised and under-funded groups, were quickly discovered and the retribution of the government was swift and violent.

Jeremy Pearson had his own small group but all they did, in fact all they could do, at that stage, was to bide their time.

He had quickly realised, after the election that swept the WDL to power, that he had personally met the new Chancellor of the Exchequer, Jacob (Jack) Rothberg. Jeremy agonised on how a man who claimed to be a good Jew, could be associated with these people? He quickly remembered the evening visit to recruit him to the Jewish Council for Democracy and he wondered, had he joined, if the WDL would have then tried to involve him in their now so obvious plans to hold on to power, come what may. He shuddered at the idea.

The days of universal international travel were over. Apart from the senior party members no one was allowed or could afford holidays, abroad or at home. There was still business travel but only for those who genuinely needed to visit suppliers and customers out of the UK. And then, before travel permits were issued, applicants were carefully investigated and only those who were loyal party members were allowed to fly out. As a result the major airports ran on skeleton staffs which were more than enough to cope with the small number of planes arriving and leaving each day. Tourism had ceased. Europe and America had their own problems but they were at least being dealt with in a democratic way. No one in their right minds wanted to visit the police state that the UK had tragically become. In any case, the government kept a tight grip on the borders to ensure no undesirables (in their eyes) could enter or leave. All ferry terminals were closed to passengers and only authorised trucks, driven by party members delivering exports, could leave or arrive on the once a day ferries. The Channel Tunnel with its high speed rail links to the continent, was sealed off. The government also increased the coastguard service to many times its original size to stop people they described as 'trouble makers' from landing on the shores of Britain.

The people were becoming more and more desperate. There was just enough food to avoid total starvation and the health of the nation was deteriorating. All over the country there were men and women who not only detested the regime (apart from the party members, everyone did) but who were determined to somehow restore democratic government. However, all landlines were monitored and most mobile networks had been closed down. Computers were only allowed to senior party members and approved businesses. To try to circumvent any of these rules was to risk your life particularly with the re-introduction of the death penalty for 'treason.'

The prisons had become so full of political prisoners that other arrangements had to be made to house the large numbers that the government considered subversive and therefore to be kept under lock and key. As a result they embarked on a large programme of building detention centres for prisoners considered a security risk. Some were old schools and hospitals and any building that could be made secure was transformed in this way.

The Security Council of the United Nations received requests for a debate on the ever deteriorating situation in Britain. However, the UK delegate exercised his veto and the USA and Russia both abstained. They had more than enough economic problems of their own to deal with. In fact America was becoming increasingly isolationist and could no longer afford to be the world's policeman.

It was a pitch-black, freezing-cold November night in the third year of the WDL government. Most street lights were now turned off at nine o'clock in the evening, partially to save cost and also because this was the time when the national curfew started. Very few people, apart from senior party members and business men, now had cars. Petrol was rationed and the price was fixed by the government at £20 per gallon. During the hours of daylight people either walked or cycled. There were limited public transport systems in the large cities to transport those going to and from work, but these were infrequent and unreliable.

Rabbi Jeremy Pearson and his wife and children lived on Jenkins Avenue, Prestwich; a quiet street of Victorian terraces. It was eleven o'clock in the evening and Miriam and the children were safely tucked up in bed. Jeremy sat at his desk, his head in his hands, as he contemplated the way they now lived. It was a Thursday night and he knew he must prepare his sermon for Saturday morning. The synagogue would be packed. It always was these days. He often wondered why, when theatres and cinemas had long since been closed down, houses of prayer were still allowed to function. He remembered how Karl Marx had attacked religion as the 'opium of the masses.' This government, so similar to the Soviets of the time of Stalin, instead of banning organised worship, had encouraged it. No doubt they saw it as a way of releasing the pressure that built up in the people during their weekdays. However, it was tightly controlled and Jeremy knew better than to use the Synagogue for any overtly or covertly political purpose.

Suddenly Jeremy's ears picked up a sound from the street outside. It sounded like someone coming up the garden path. Then he heard a gentle tapping first on the front door and then on the window. *Who would dare to be out at this time of night?* he wondered. He pondered on whether he should open the front door. If it was the police to complain about something in last week's sermon, they would hardly conceal their arrival. They would bang on the door. He remembered last year when Jim Murphy, a Liberal-Democrat councillor who lived just down the street, had been arrested. That was after midnight and the arresting officers had arrived to a fanfare of sirens. When the tapping was repeated a third time, Jeremy decided to open the door but with the chain still in place.

"Who is it?" he whispered through the small opening.

"My name is Andrew Robertson and I need to talk to you," was the whispered reply.

"What do you want?" Jeremy replied suspiciously. "You know there is a curfew."

"Look Rabbi," Robertson continued. "Can I come in. I need to see you. I am from Worsley. I have come a long way specially."

Jeremy considered the request. The man was well spoken, obviously educated and desperate to see him. He did not appear to be Jewish – to his knowledge there were few if any Jews in Worsley. Certainly there was no Synagogue. The requested meeting was probably for a political purpose and that was dangerous. The man had broken the curfew to visit him and that was foolhardy. However, Jeremy decided to take a risk and let the stranger enter. He quietly closed the door, unhooked the chain and re-opened to allow Robertson to enter. Jeremy quickly surveyed the visitor. He was a similar height to the Rabbi, just under six feet. He was well built although, like most people nowadays, he looked a little haggard as if a really good meal would not go amiss. He had piercing blue eyes and by way of thanks he treated Jeremy to a dazzling smile. He had light sandy hair turning grey at the temples and he was dressed in the universal uniform of jeans and a sweater that had obviously seen better days. Despite the cold outside, he wore no coat.

The pair shook hands solemnly in the hall and Jeremy ushered the man into his study.

"A nice hot cup of tea or coffee?" Jeremy enquired. "You must be frozen!"

"Yes please," Andrew replied, again showing his dazzling smile. "That would be wonderful."

"I am also going to bring in some of my wife's freshly baked Swiss Roll for you."

"You are very kind," Andrew commented.

It took a few minutes to boil up the kettle and to cut a few slices of Swiss Roll and when Jeremy returned to the study he found Andrew slumped in a chair and fast-asleep.

The poor fellow must be exhausted, Jeremy decided and covered his guest with a blanket.

After about ten minutes the visitor awoke and apologised for dozing off.

"Don't worry!" Jeremy assured him. "The combined effects of the long walk and the cold must have made you drowsy."

"Well actually, I did not come from Worsley tonight. I do live there but tonight I came here from Didsbury," Andrew explained.

"That is quite a walk," Jeremy commented.

He liked this man. He seemed to be direct and trustworthy but Jeremy knew of many people who had been befriended by strangers who had betrayed them as soon as there was a hint of objection or criticism of the tyrannical government under whom they lived.

"So, Andrew," Jeremy began. "What can I do for you?"

"I am taking a big chance in coming to you but I used to enjoy your interviews on TV and radio on matters of personal conduct and morality," Andrew explained. "I do not believe that a man like you could be happy with our present government."

Jeremy surveyed the man sitting opposite him. He seemed to be sincere but the Rabbi only needed to agree with Andrew's last statement and if he was a government spy, all would be lost.

"Do you know the penalties for speaking out, even privately against the government?" He enquired.

"Yes and I thought you would need to be convinced of my sincerity," Andrew replied.

He fished into his pocket and produced a somewhat crumpled A4 sheet which he handed to the Rabbi.

It was headed,

Voices in the Wilderness.
The Newsletter of the re-Birth of Democracy Movement.
Editor: Andrew Robertson

Jeremy started to read the short news items which mainly told brief stories of brave men and women who had dared to stand up to the authorities. In every case, Jeremy observed, they had finished up in prison.

"You do realise that if you were caught on the street with this, you could actually be tried for treason and shot?" Jeremy enquired.

"Of course," Andrew replied, "but I needed some tangible evidence, however flimsy, to try and convince you of my bona fides. Now you have seen this, please destroy it. If you wish to go into your backyard to burn it, I will come with you to make sure there is nothing left of such an incriminating document."

Jeremy took up the man's suggestion and they watched the flames quickly devour the primitive news-sheet.

As soon as the two men returned to Jeremy's study, Jeremy repeated the question he had asked when Andrew arrived.

"What can I do for you?"

"My organisation is appointing men and women in all major towns and cities to become leaders of groups who will eventually take back this country from the evil people who are now running it. We know all about your background and we would like you to become one of our leaders in this area."

"Look, Andrew," the Rabbi quickly decided to take a chance and agree with the visitor's last statement about the government. "I detest this regime just as much as you do but what chance do we have? The police, the army, the judges, local government, even the church are now totally controlled by government nominees."

"Listen to me Jeremy," Andrew explained. "We are not complete idiots. Do you think I am crazy? None of us has a death wish and we know that this is a long term programme. At the moment we are just at the beginning of the planning stage. Are you in? All I want tonight is a commitment that when the time comes you will be one of the brave people who will organise resistance in Greater Manchester."

"Andrew," Jeremy ventured. "I am neither a soldier nor a politician, I am what you Christians call a man of the cloth. What use am I in what you are trying to achieve?"

"I told you before that you had been selected because of your background. We know you were brought up in this city and that you obtained a first class law degree in Birmingham. We even know that your dissatisfaction with the religion of your birth led you to convert to Judaism. That in itself is unusual and to then become a Rabbi is truly remarkable. We are not looking for violent men but we are looking for intelligent men who care deeply about their fellows. That is why I risked my life tonight to come here to see you."

"May I discuss this with my wife before giving you an answer?" Jeremy enquired. "Look," he continued, "I cannot let you go out again tonight. You must stay here until the curfew is lifted at dawn. If you agree I will speak to Miriam before you leave in the morning."

Andrew nodded. "Of course you must discuss this whole matter with your wife. Obviously she was also profiled and we are confident that she must feel broken-hearted about what has happened to her country. I would then be pleased to add some further explanations of my own to you both. As for staying until morning, I can sleep on the couch and I was hoping you would suggest this," he finished with another smile.

"Just one more thing," Jeremy added gravely.

"What is that?" Andrew replied looking a little concerned.

"Would you like another cup of tea?"

Chapter eighteen

A Man with a Plan

Miriam and Jeremy were early risers except on the Sabbath (Saturday) when there was no school and Synagogue prayers did not start until 9.15.

The morning after Andrew's visit was Friday. Miriam came downstairs at half past six and went straight into the kitchen to prepare breakfast. With a large pan of porridge gently bubbling on the hob and the electric kettle beginning to boil, she followed her usual morning routine of opening the curtains in the ground floor rooms before returning upstairs to persuade her children to leave their nice warm beds. As she entered the study she flicked on the light switch. At this time of the year it would still be dark. She was wondering what time her husband had come to bed. She never heard him enter the bedroom or slide himself silently under the sheets. *It must have been very late*, she decided. She marched across the room and flung open the curtains. Just then she heard her husband's footsteps noisily, heavily and quickly running down the creaky staircase. *Why is he coming down now?* She brooded. *He will wake the children before I am ready for them.* She turned round to leave the room and then she saw the figure of a man, still sleeping, stretched out on the couch. Miriam would have been shocked by her discovery but Jeremy's arrival overtook any chance of concern that she might have had.

"It's alright Miriam," he shouted as he entered the room. "I did not want you to find him before I had the chance to tell you about our visitor."

Of course Jeremy's noisy entry into the study awoke Andrew with a start.

"Miriam," the Rabbi continued. "This is Andrew Robertson. He arrived late last night on a dangerous mission. We will explain all after breakfast."

Miriam stared at Andrew and realising her bad manners said,

"Err! welcome Mr Robertson."

Andrew gave her a somewhat watery smile.

"Come Miriam," Jeremy suggested. "Let us leave Mr Robertson to come round properly."

Turning to Andrew he explained that there was a shower in the washroom under the stairs and he would find clean towels in a cupboard.

"Obviously you do not have a change of clothing. You are however, luckily about the same size as I am. I will loan you some of mine."

"Really Jeremy," Andrew replied, "this is too much. I am becoming a major inconvenience."

"Nonsense," Jeremy answered. "None of this is a problem. What we have to discuss is far more of a problem!"

Before Miriam returned upstairs to see to the children, Jeremy ushered her into the kitchen and quickly explained the reason for Andrew's visit. She was understandably horrified.

"Are you crazy?" she demanded. "As soon as a few people find out about what we are doing, we will be reported and that will be the end of us. You know that we now live in a police state. Have you forgotten what happened to our neighbour Jim Murphy?"

"If a man like Andrew Robertson can risk his life in travelling around the country, I believe it is up to us to do our bit to rid Britain of this tyrannical government. Miriam," he continued. "Do you think the Maccabbees hesitated when they needed to rid Israel of the evil men who were controlling their lives? And what about Moshe Rabeinu (Moses?) Did he hesitate when God told him to demand freedom for his people from Pharaoh?"

Miriam nodded but was far from convinced. She was a wife and a mother and her first thoughts were for the safety of her family.

"Well," she said uncertainly, with a sick feeling in the pit of her stomach, "we had better hear what this man has to say."

Andrew was still showering and Jeremy said his morning prayers. Normally he would have gone to Synagogue but with their visitor to be given breakfast, and for the three of them to discuss last night's conversation, he prayed at home.

Jeremy decided that it would be prudent not to let the children see that they had a visitor. They might mention it at school where a one or two of the senior teachers were loyal members of the WDL. So Jeremy waited with Andrew in the study with the door firmly closed, until the children had left.

The men then had their breakfast and chatted, not without difficulty, about inconsequential matters. The conversation, of course, was rather forced as what they both wanted to discuss had to await the return of Miriam from seeing the children safely into school.

It was a quarter to ten when Miriam eventually returned. One of the teachers had wanted to talk to her about extra lessons for Yitzi.

So, somewhat behind schedule the three of them sat down in the study.

"So, I hope you are now going to tell me properly what this is all about," Miriam ventured. "The Rabbi has told me the little he knows and I have to say it all sounds incredibly dangerous."

"Of course, my dear," the Rabbi replied.

He then proceeded to explain the purpose of Andrew's visit, with a few minor points of clarification from their guest.

Miriam sat staring at her husband throughout the entire presentation. When he had finished she said, in a voice heavy with emotion,

"This is absolute madness, you know."

Then Andrew spoke.

"What we are trying to do is a task so overwhelming that quite frankly it terrifies me. We are, throughout the UK, less than a thousand people but if we are to get our country back from this Sidney Charleston and his henchmen a start must be made now."

Miriam looked at him as if he had just been discharged from a mental institution.

"And how do you propose that we do that?" she enquired.

"Do you know how Charleston and his gang organised the takeover?"

Jeremy and Miriam shook their heads.

"With one initial group of fifteen people with the same distorted view of the world that he had. They had to recruit fifteen people each and then they, the next group, had to recruit another fifteen people. It only took five levels, rather like pyramid selling for over three quarters of a million people to be recruited. They however, had one huge advantage; the internet. Now of course, computers are only allowed to party members and for industry, commerce and the government. There is total control over them and most websites operating from abroad are blocked. However," Andrew continued, "the principal of pyramid selling can still be applied without computers."

Rabbi and Mrs Pearson both regarded the visitor in amazement.

"How is that possible?" Jeremy enquired.

"We each need to contact fifteen people on whom we are totally certain we can rely. If there is the slightest doubt and you have even the tiniest suspicion that they may be government supporters, leave well alone."

"Ok," Jeremy enquired. "Assuming that can be done and it is a big assumption, we then need to document their names or at least a way of contacting them. Then what happens?"

"We need literally millions of people, not just an initial three quarters of a million, like them. If just one supporter of the regime gets wind of this at the beginning, the whole thing could be blown sky high. We need to be absolutely certain about our initial contacts. What is vital is that none of us should ever know the identities of people further down the line. I am sure tragic mistakes will be made and some wrong people will be approached, but that way no more than seventeen people could ever be compromised. They would be the original recruiter, the man or woman approached to build a group and their fifteen members. Are you sure I have made all this clear for you?"

Jeremy and Miriam both nodded a little uncertainly.

"So," Jeremy replied, "Let us assume I can find and recruit fifteen people who hate this evil government. That should not be difficult. I then tell each of them to recruit another fifteen people of their own. Fine," he continued, "but what is the purpose of all this?"

"Then will come the crunch," Andrew explained. "On a date that will be passed down the line, millions of people will leave their homes and converge on city and town centres and all government and local government offices. They will of course be walking but the sheer volume of men and women on the streets at the same time will bring all movement to a standstill. Police stations and army bases will also be included in the targets. I am sure that even the most violent uniformed people will be intimidated. A huge mass of people, as far back as the eye can see, will be terrifying, even if you are holding a gun. Sadly, there will be some fatalities from hot-headed policemen and soldiers opening fire but the surging mass of mankind will quickly overwhelm them."

"And do we tell our fifteen that this will be the ultimate goal?" Jeremy asked.

"No," replied Andrew. "At the moment all they need to know is that in six months or so they will be required to take part in a mass demonstration. When we name the time and date we will give four weeks notice for the news to be passed down and supply further details."

Jeremy looked at Miriam.

"What do you think? Would this work?"

"It all sounds far too simple to me," Miriam replied thoughtfully. "But I have to say it may be the only way of getting rid of these terrible people."

The Rabbi nodded and slowly added,

"You know, Andrew, it might just work."

"So are you both in?" Andrew enquired.

"Yes, I suppose so. This is a very dangerous journey we are starting on and we have our children to think of. However, what kind of a future can they have under the dictatorship of this Sidney Charleston and his gang."

Jeremy and Miriam sat back as if stunned into silence until the Rabbi again leaned forward and asked Andrew,

"So. Let us assume with God's help, we are successful. What happens then? So many of our politicians from the three main old political parties have been executed. Those that haven't are being imprisoned in the most appalling conditions and I am sure that their health will be broken from disease and hunger. We will need a provisional government until elections can be called."

"Activists in all fifteen major population areas are aware of this. Believe me, there are people out there waiting to take the reins. Do you remember how amazed we all were when the Soviet Union collapsed, to find educated, English speaking democrats ready to govern." Andrew confided.

"So is yours the very first group of fifteen?" Jeremy asked.

Andrew nodded and allowed himself the luxury of a smile.

"And you will be part of my group, just one level down. The question of having some sort of government in waiting has already been discussed by the first group. We saw what happened back in the Arab spring of 2011 and 2012 when they disposed of bad governments but did not have credible alternatives ready to take over. So having got rid of one tyranny, many of them found themselves governed by another group of extremists just as bad or even worse."

Andrew looked at his watch. It was now five minutes past eleven and he had anther long walk ahead of him to his next recruit.

"I will be in touch. Please start to recruit your fifteen as soon as possible. Thank you for your hospitality and I will return the clothes you lent me the next time I am in the district."

Rabbi Jeremy rose and grasped Andrew's hand.

"Please God, our deliberations will be blessed with a successful conclusion and decency and freedom will return to this land."

"Amen to that," Andrew replied as he walked briskly towards the front door of the house.

Chapter Nineteen

A Glittering Occasion

Colonel Sidney Charleston had now been living in the official residence of the British Prime Minister at 10 Downing Street for over five years. These had been turbulent years for the country and not without incident for him. He was, he felt, doing his best for his country in difficult circumstances and it troubled him that he was not appreciated more for all his efforts.

A number of senior members of his first cabinet had deserted him as the going became increasingly tough. If there was one thing he could not stand, it was disloyalty. How and why Jacob Rothberg had started to openly criticise him after the affair of the Chief Constables, he could not imagine. Didn't Jacob know he needed a completely loyal obedient police force to control all the dissidents and rioters? Old friend or not, he had to go. The only sure way to remove him from his important role of Chancellor of the Exchequer was to discredit him. The rather shady accountants the PM had employed did a wonderful job of manufacturing evidence that Rothberg had been sending large sums of public money to his own Swiss bank accounts. He was now languishing in jail. As for Ahmed Yamani, he had been stupid enough to object to the closing of the borders. In fact his behaviour was appalling. Sidney had been deeply hurt by Ahmed's outburst and the PM then had no alternative but to have him locked up as an Islamic Terror suspect.

Thank heavens, Sidney thought, Angus Ferguson, the Secretary of State for Home Affairs, knew how to conduct himself. Sidney was grateful to him for sorting out the loyal police chiefs from the trouble makers. He was certainly one cabinet member the PM could rely on.

It had been a shame that John Pilkington had objected to the trials of the three party leaders. Anyway, he was now in jail for 'bribing jurors.' Most of the other members of his original cabinet had stood the test of time. Strangely enough, not one of the women had caused any trouble. They and the remaining men seemed to go along with all Sidney's rules without demur. However it had been an excellent idea to take on the portfolios of Foreign Affairs and the Exchequer himself. The newly appointed civil servants, permanent secretaries of those departments, advised him well and carried out his instructions to the letter.

The Prime Minister's personal life also had not all been smooth sailing. It was sad that Daphne had discovered his affair with Justine Fletcher, his secretary. What had possessed Daphne to enter his office without knocking just as he and Justine were about to get dressed after one of their little daily sessions, he would never know. However, Justine was definitely worth it. He had never achieved the level of personal gratification with Daphne that Justine gave him. The trouble was that Daphne's father, that old devil Charles Craigwell-Smyth, had tried to make trouble for him and cause a public scandal. However, one of the bright new detective sergeants that the new Commissioner of the Met had recruited had planted the body of an old tramp in Charles' car boot and he was now serving a life sentence for murder.

Sidney now never left the country. He owed it to the UK to take great care of himself. His security detail of fifty sharp-shooting bodyguards surrounded him at all times when away from Downing Street on state business. There was, of course no reason to visit the Palace of Westminster as parliament had been suspended indefinitely under the state of emergency. He did, however regularly visit the provinces to show support for the city mayors. They were all, without exception, good, loyal party members and the sort of money they were making, with his blessing, ensured that they were with him to a man.

The Mayor of Greater Manchester was Thomas Appleby. He had been an Assistant Governor at Strangeways Prison when he applied for the newly created position. He was heartily detested by prisoners and staff alike because of his aggressive, domineering attitude. He had been sent to London for an interview and it came as a profound shock to him to find he was to be interviewed personally by Angus Ferguson, the Home Secretary.

"You do realise, Thomas, may I call you Thomas?" Angus had said, "the north-west is one of the most important regions in the country and we must have a man there who will be one hundred percent committed to Colonel Charleston and the WDL. If you are appointed you will have a free hand in maintaining law and order. If there is riot or insurrection you may tell your men to shoot first and ask questions afterwards. We for our part will not be asking questions. Just keep the trouble makers under control."

The Home Secretary already knew that Thomas Appleby had frequently been summoned to explain why prisoners on his watch had been killed or seriously injured when they stepped out of line.

Thomas, of course, was ideal and along with similar men appointed to these top positions in cities such as London, Glasgow, Liverpool, Birmingham, Newcastle, Bristol and Nottingham, he was invited to meet the Prime Minister personally, to confirm his appointment before returning home.

It was May and the Prime Minister was on tour. After spending two days in Birmingham, he and his entourage set off for Manchester. He was welcomed into the city by the Mayor, Thomas Appleby, and escorted under the usual tight security to the Town Hall for a lavish luncheon. Sidney had brought his new wife, Justine, with him. She was hosted by the Mayor's wife, Barbara. Like so many of the WDL functionaries, she had had a somewhat checkered career. She was a tall well built blonde who believed in flashing most of her not inconsiderable assets in low cut dresses and blouses. These attributes had served her well in her earlier career as a night-club hostess. It was there that she had met her husband. On the other hand Justine, the Prime Minister's lady, was petite, dark haired and naturally pretty. She also spoke and acted like a lady other than when she was alone with her husband. That, of course, was not subject to public scrutiny.

The Mayor wanted to show the Prime Minister how he was taming the various ethnic groups that went to make up the population of this metropolis. After careful vetting, representatives of a number of different groups were invited. They included Mao Chu Lai of the Chinese community; Ismail Mansour of the Sunni Mosque in Prestwich, David Levine, a prominent member of the Jewish community and a number of well known churchmen from the Roman Catholic, Church of England and Methodist groups. In addition, a large representative group of industrialists, bankers and businessmen were invited. All of these latter people, without exception, were members of the WDL and Thomas Appleby had instructed his staff to investigate if any of those present had ever, publicly criticised the government or shown signs of dissent. Needless to say they had all passed scrutiny and were considered suitable to be in attendance at a function graced by the Prime Minister.

In accordance with protocol the Mayor, Thomas Appleby, stood at the door of the large hall to greet the guests and introduce them to the distinguished visitor. As the guests filed past they shook hands with Sidney Charleston. Some, the few who had previously met him and were probably party activists, exchanged a few words. Then a strange thing happened.

David Levine of the Jewish community shook hands with the Mayor and was introduced to the Prime Minister. He extended his hand and then said,

"Excuse me Sir, but have we met before?"

"No Mr Levine," Sidney replied. "I certainly do not recall a previous meeting."

"You seem so familiar to me," Levine continued.

Sidney Charleston was never blessed with much patience and in any case this David Levine was holding up the queue.

"Look Mr Levine, Sorry! I don't know you and you are holding up the line. Please move on."

David reluctantly strolled into the banqueting hall and found his place at the table. However, throughout the luncheon and subsequent speeches he kept looking at the Prime Minister. And then suddenly he realised; he was a double of his Rabbi, Jeremy Pearson. The Rabbi of course had a beard but the height, figure and colouring were all identical. Even the dark hair was the same. And the eyes; it was the eyes that first alerted him to the similarity. Then the Prime Minister rose to speak. He spoke in the clipped tones of a military man and his vowel sounds were definitely southern. The Rabbi, on the other hand had a slight Manchester accent. However, the timbre of the voices was alarmingly close. David Levine was puzzled. How could this be? As the Prime Minister's speech drew to a close David realised that he had not absorbed a word of what Charleston had said. But that hardly mattered. David heartily disliked the man and his government. He quite understandably, like any right-thinking person, considered them to be a bunch of thugs who had somehow hijacked the country. However, like the majority of the population, he was far too prudent and afraid, yes he was afraid, to voice any criticism in public. He knew what happened to people who did. They finished up either in jail or even worse, they finished up having most unfortunate fatal 'accidents.'

David had been quite surprised to receive the Mayor's invitation and after just a few minutes discussion with his wife, they agreed that it would be imprudent to refuse. Now he was here in the Town Hall, the President of a major Synagogue and shocked to discover such a strong physical similarity between two men. One of them, he detested and the other he loved. *How strange life could be,* he pondered.

CHAPTER TWENTY

AN UNCANNY RESEMBLANCE

Finding fifteen people who they knew hated the Prime Minister, his government and supporters was easy. Finding fifteen people who were the souls of discretion and reliability was a little more difficult. Each one had to be vetted carefully by Jeremy and Miriam. The desperate necessity to maintain confidentiality and secrecy was vital. The candidates needed to know that at some time in the future there would be a huge demonstration against the government. They needed to be reminded that they would be acting against the laws enshrined in the continuing state of emergency. These stated quite clearly that any assembly of more than four people, on the streets, was illegal. Everyone knew that innocent members of the public had been shot dead for less. The tightly controlled press, naturally, never reported these shootings as anything other than the destruction by the security forces of 'terrorist plots.' Finally the candidates for the Pearson's fifteen had to assure them that they could appoint another fifteen people of their own and do so in a similar manner to their own interview. Secrecy was absolutely essential.

It took the best part of a month to choose and enrol their fifteen and when it was done they agonised over whether they had made any mistakes with their choices. As a well-known Rabbi of a large Synagogue Jeremy knew literally hundreds of people. Also, his work with other faith leaders over the years, had made him large numbers of other contacts outside the Jewish community. Some of these political ones, from the old Town councils were no longer around. If they had been determined democrats and objected vociferously from the start to the dictatorial ways of the new national government, they were either in prison or dead. Anyway the task of finding the fifteen was completed and it became their turn to find their own reliable groups of contacts. The Rabbi had been obliged to warn the majority of his fifteen that, they or certainly their own individual groups would need to look outside the Jewish community if duplication of personnel was to be avoided.

The second person enrolled by Jeremy had been the current president of his Synagogue, David Levine. He had recently attended a luncheon given by the Mayor to honour the Prime Minister on a visit to Manchester. David had been horrified by the way this government and especially its leader Sidney Charleston had deliberately set out to overturn the British tradition of democracy and to cruelly destroy all opposition to their plans. Had he not had the common sense to maintain a low profile, he would not only have forfeited the invitation to meet the PM but almost certainly have forfeited his liberty and quite possibly his life as well.

When approached by the Rabbi he was initially reluctant to become involved.

"Rabbi, you do realise we are risking our lives in what looks like a venture that is highly unlikely to succeed," he commented. He was not a coward but he found it difficult to believe that the plan that Jeremy had described, could possibly have any but a tragic ending. However, he felt that if the Rabbi was involved he had better, at least agree to be included, and then see if these groups of fifteen could be enrolled. So, the day after committing himself David set about finding his own fifteen people. Jeremy had advised him to look outside their own community and as a lawyer in the city he had many contacts across all the ethnic and religious communities that made up the population of the county. Some of these contacts he knew were at best unreliable and at worst party members of the WDL so he had to tread very carefully. However, among his new group were five of his own partners who he knew he could trust. There were two others in the firm who he suspected, for their own reasons, were supporters of the party. It was significant that when the Town Hall needed solicitors, these two were usually instructed. For some time he had been suspicious of them and was convinced that they were being paid far more for their services than appeared in their bills. However, once again David held his peace. What possible good would it do to accuse two of his partners of accepting corrupt payments from the Mayor's office. This was how the whole country was being run; by a combination of tyranny and corruption.

David was still brooding about the remarkable physical similarity between the Prime Minister and his Rabbi. When he reported back to Jeremy that his fifteen were now firmly in place, he raised the matter with him.

"Rabbi, I don't think I told you that when I went to the luncheon in honour of our 'wonderful' Prime Minister the other week," he said with heavy irony, "I was quite taken aback by the strong physical similarity he has to you."

The Rabbi knew all about this. The first time this had been suggested had been when Jacob Rothberg had said something similar to him when he called upon him that night, now some seven or eight years ago.

"Yes, David, it is not the first time that comment has been made," he replied with a sigh.

"I would hope that is where the similarity begins and ends. I have no desire to resemble such an evil man, in any way."

"Of course not, Rabbi," David replied, determined not to let the subject rest. "However, have you never noticed it yourself when watching television?"

"I do not often watch television. Of course I listen to the radio and read the newspapers, although these days that is a waste of time as they are all heavily censored."

"You must have seen his photograph plastered all over the newspapers" David continued. "Did you never notice the similarity?"

Of course the Rabbi had noticed but it was hardly something he was proud of. He knew he had been adopted and he tried to close his mind to even the remotest possibility that he may somehow be related to the tyrant, Charleston.

"Look David," he explained. "Of course I know there is a physical similarity but in view of his behaviour, I prefer not to be reminded of this painful fact at every end and turn."

He had discussed this matter secretly, with his wife Miriam, on many occasions. She no longer mentioned it to him as she knew how much it distressed him.

David Levine now realised that this whole subject was a frequent source of aggravation to Jeremy and he promised himself never to raise it again.

However, there were others who had already decided that, when the time was right, this similarity of appearance could be used to advantage.

CHAPTER TWENTY ONE

A REQUEST AND A REFUSAL

Just six weeks had elapsed since the visit of Andrew Robertson. He was frequently in Jeremy's thoughts. He recognised him as a decent man fighting against tremendous odds to wrest the country from the stranglehold of the WDL. The Rabbi had discovered some time ago that the original name of the party had been the Western Democratic League and what a complete misnomer this had become.

It was a Shabbat (Saturday) and as usual the Synagogue was fairly full with a congregation, many of whom were showing serious signs of the strain they were living under. They prayed with an intensity that in better days Jeremy would have found both satisfying and surprising. Now they were praying for food, work and to have the yoke of the WDL oppressor lifted from their lives. Somehow, most of them were getting by, but life was far from sweet.

It was during the sermon that the Rabbi noticed a stranger sitting at the very back of Synagogue. When this happened the visitor was usually one of a number of members of the WDL who were sent to visit Mosques on Fridays, Synagogues on Saturday and Churches on Sunday. Their job was to ensure that the congregations were not hearing any kind of negative comments from their preachers, about the government. This stranger was wearing a thirties-style rain-hat which all but obscured his face. Jeremy finished his sermon being extra careful not to say anything that could be misconstrued and taken as a political statement. As he came down from the pulpit he glanced again at the visitor and realised that it was Andrew Robertson. It was now time for silent prayer and Jeremy noticed that Andrew had picked up a prayer-book and was pretending to pray in the same manner as the other people round him. Jeremy was sure Andrew did not read Hebrew and the Rabbi was momentarily amused to see the effort Andrew was making to fit in.

After the service it was the custom of the congregation to line up to greet the Rabbi, Cantor and honorary officials by wishing them a Good Shabbos (Sabbath) or Shabbat Shalom, the Hebrew term. Jeremy wondered what Andrew would do and eventually noticed him hanging back to be the last in the queue.

When his turn came he gave a hearty handshake to the line-up of officials and offered a quite convincing, 'Good Shabbos!'

The President, David Levine and one of the wardens tried to engage him in conversation and were rewarded with a muttered 'Just Visiting' explanation.

When he reached the Rabbi at the end of the line Jeremy greeted him with a smile.

"Good Shabbos, Andrew," he said, as if this was the most natural place in the world for Andrew to appear. "Nice to see you here. Do you want to chat?"

Andrew, of course, nodded and the pair made their way to the Rabbi's private study.

Once they were seated in the small room, Jeremy explained that after the Synagogue service it was usual to make a celebratory public blessing of the Sabbath. This was called Kiddush and after the short prayer it was traditional to have a glass of wine, to complete the short ceremony. However, Jeremy explained, when the public hall of the congregation was being used for a private celebration, maybe for a Barmitzvah or forthcoming wedding, members of the community made Kiddush at home, with their families. Fortunately that day there was no communal Kiddush, Jeremy explained.

"However, I will make Kiddush first," he told Andrew, "before we chat."

The Rabbi poured out two small glasses of red wine and proceeded to make the blessing. When Andrew sipped his, he found it rather sweet for his taste but rather than offend Jeremy, he drank the small amount, but not without an involuntary shudder.

"I gather that did not go down too well," Jeremy commented with a smile. "I do have a small amount of Whisky if you would like a chaser."

Most forms of liquor had become prohibitively expensive and Jeremy had been keeping this bottle for some unspecified special occasion. However, much to his relief, Andrew declined the offer.

"Right," said the Rabbi. "Now what can I do for you?"

Andrew stood up again and put a finger to his lips to indicate to Jeremy to be silent. He took an electronic device from out of his pocket. Jeremy then realised that Andrew needed to 'sweep' the entire room to be certain there were no listening devices installed. He nodded to his guest and Andrew began his task. Although the room was small it took the best part of five minutes to complete the task. Eventually, Andrew nodded.

"Ok," he began as he sat once again in the comfortable arm-chair opposite the Rabbi.

"I have two matters to discuss with you. One of them is quite straight forward and is simply to question how the formation of your fifteen has gone?"

"Well," Jeremy replied. "My fifteen have been selected and I believe they are all people I can rely upon. By now they should have chosen their own fifteens and indeed, hopefully, the recruitments at further levels are proceeding well."

"Well, I can't ask for more than that at this stage," Andrew replied.

"The other matter I have to deal with is even more dangerous; in fact far, far more dangerous," he continued.

"What is that?" Jeremy asked, wondering what Andrew was about to ask of him now.

"I may as well come straight out with it," Andrew replied. "We need you to impersonate the Prime Minister."

Jeremy was not often bereft of the power of speech. Communicating through words was his business. However, he just sat there in stunned silence surveying Andrew across his desk.

Andrew had hoped for some reaction from the Rabbi but Jeremy simply sat and stared at him as if he had gone mad.

Finally Andrew decided to continue.

"I realise this request must come as something of a shock to you but this is really important."

Suddenly the Rabbi re-located his tongue and other speech equipment.

"Look Andrew, you know I am one hundred per cent with you. I detest Mr Charleston and this government just as much as you do. When you came out of the blue, and asked me to start a network of fifteen, I agreed and I will continue to facilitate this process. However, what you are now asking me is absolutely out of the question. Please do not try to give me details of how your crazy plan would work. I am a Rabbi not some kind of James Bond character. I am not the right man for this escapade."

Andrew looked totally crestfallen. He knew Jeremy would be hardly likely to jump at the opportunity. It was a very dangerous plan but nevertheless he felt that if it was explained to Jeremy, there was a chance that he would agree. However, if he was refusing to even hear the details, Andrew's mission would be a failure.

"Can I not just explain an outline of the plan to you?" he asked.

"No,!" Jeremy answered. "You have the wrong man for this job. If you have a serious idea about what looks to me like a hair-brained scheme, you need someone who is really skilled in acting and subterfuge."

"I came to you because you have one huge advantage over everyone else; you strongly resemble friend Charleston."

"I am well-aware of that but I am still not the right man for this job," the Rabbi replied with finality.

"Please may I wish you and your associates every success in all you are trying do to rid us of this tyrant and now I must return home to make Kiddush for my family."

Jeremy stood up and offered a warm handshake to the deeply disappointed Andrew.

"I pray that God will bless your enterprise and all you are doing with success."

Andrew managed a watery smile and the two men walked silently out of the side door of the synagogue.

Chapter Twenty two

Tragedy

Miriam, Jeremy's wife was the daughter of Rabbi Goldfine, a saintly man who spent his time in Gateshead teaching young men in considerable detail, the finest points about their faith. He was a world authority on Jewish law and as such, was consulted by other Rabbis and learned men from all over the world.

It was a warm spring day in April and Jeremy had been able to borrow a car from a member of the congregation who was allowed the vehicle for business travel. This was the only way they could travel with their children to Gateshead to see Miriam's parents. He had also obtained a permit to travel, from the Manchester Town Hall. He explained that he was taking his family with him for a refresher course at his old college in north eastern England and the necessary permit was granted. The cost of the petrol was astronomically expensive and they could only afford this trip once each year.

This was the third year in succession that they had made the journey. Jeremy knew that if he drove on lesser known roads and avoided the towns and cities, they should have an uneventful journey. They had been stopped at police and army road blocks in the two previous years and then waved through when his permit was shown. This year was tragically destined to be very different.

They were high up traversing the bleak desolate moors that divide Lancashire from Yorkshire when Jeremy saw ahead of him an army check-point. He made to slow down to speak to the soldiers when his youngest, Shlomo, just two years old, wriggled free of his car seat, jumped on the rear seat of the vehicle and grabbed his father from behind. Jeremy had no idea this was about to happen and he jerked his body causing him to press down hard on the accelerator. The car lurched forward and one of the soldiers, thinking they were about to drive through the road block, opened fire. The car crashed against a heavy concrete barrier but fortunately did not catch fire. The three boys in the back were screaming and shouting, Jeremy was momentarily stunned but quickly re-gained consciousness. The car was now surrounded by young, inexperienced soldiers who were pointing their rifles menacingly at the occupants of the vehicle. Jeremy opened the door to be met by a rifle muzzle.

"Get out of the car," the nearest soldier yelled, "with your hands high above your head." Jeremy complied.

At that moment a senior officer arrived from the other direction.

"What is going on here?" he demanded.

"These people were trying to crash through the barrier," one of the soldiers explained.

"What are they, dissidents?" the officer demanded.

"Sure just look at this one with his beard, probably a disguise."

Then the officer heard the three children crying in the back of the crashed car.

He turned in fury on the soldier,

"I can hear little children crying in the back of the car. What are they, also dissidents?"

Suddenly Jeremy realised that his wife Miriam was making no attempt to calm the children.

"Sir," he addressed the officer. "My wife is very quiet in the front of the car, can I see if she is alright?"

"Yes," replied the officer quietly, "go with the soldier round to the other side of the car and get her and the children out of there."

A few seconds later Jeremy was opening the front passenger door of the car and looking at the fixed stare of his beloved wife with a neat bullet hole in the centre of her forehead.

He knew instantly that she was dead but almost hysterically tried to shake her inert body back to life. Then he collapsed onto the ground sobbing.

The soldier also knew that she was dead and he knew that he was the one who had panicked and fired the shot that had snuffed out her young life.

He called over the top of the car to the officer,

"Sir, the woman is dead."

The officer immediately marched round to the passenger side of the wrecked car and confirmed for himself that this poor young woman had had her life snuffed out by one of these stupid boys who did not deserve to be dignified with the description of soldiers.

The husband was, very understandably, in a terrible state. He had pulled himself up and was simply holding the open car door and weeping as he surveyed the body of his beloved Miriam.

The officer opened the rear door and ushered the three little boys out of the car. They were all terrified and crying and he gently escorted them over to his own vehicle stopped at the other side of the road block. Fortunately he had been giving Sergeant Rosemary Jenkinson a lift back to base and he told her to look after the children. He then returned to the crash and the distraught husband and father.

On this particular morning the officer was on his way back to the garrison after a few days leave. He was horrified when he saw what had just occurred at the check-point. One of these young idiots had opened fire and killed the wife of this man. Jeremy was dressed in his normal 'off duty' clothing of a sweater and jeans. Only the beard was a little unusual but then more and more members of the British public were growing beards. It was somehow a subtle protest against what had happened to their lives. Then the officer spotted the skull-cap on the Rabbi's head.

Alongside the road-block was a hut where the soldiers sat and drank tea and played card games to break the boredom of such a lonely watch. The officer gently lead Jeremy to the hut where he seated him on one of the hard stools that constituted the only furniture other than a small table.

"Are you Jewish?" the officer gently enquired.

Jeremy nodded.

"Will you have a cup of tea?" he continued.

"Yes, but without milk," the Rabbi replied tearfully.

"Are you able to tell me what happened?" the officer said.

Jeremy nodded his head and proceeded to tell the officer the whole tragic story. This was punctuated with sobs but he knew this man who seemed to be so kind, must be told the entire chain of events that had led to him losing his wife and helpmate.

Captain Martin Benson had been in the army for twenty years. He was a veteran of the Iraq and Afghanistan campaigns and had been decorated for bravery. He had also served under the man who was now the dictator of Britain, Colonel Sidney Charleston and had originally been grateful to him for recommending Martin for promotion. However, once Charleston had retired from the army he had started to see a totally different side to the man. He watched his old Commanding Officer becoming the head of a new political party and then being voted into government, quite democratically with a huge parliamentary majority. He then watched his old C.O. dispense with all the democratic institutions one by one and install his own cronies, people who could be paid handsomely to co-operate with the new government in terrorising the population into submission.

As far as the Prime Minister was concerned Captain Benson was completely reliable. He knew him personally and was sure that his assistance in Martin's military career was appreciated. Charleston therefore had no doubts about the loyalty of the captain. This was where he had made a mistake. Captain Benson was disgusted by the behaviour of his former mentor and originally wanted to leave the army and somehow escape abroad. However, after observing the way that the new upper echelons of the police and army, many of them former criminals, were treating the population he decided that he must stay, retain a low profile and try to help the people whenever the opportunity presented itself. As a result, on a number of occasions, he had stopped his own troops from opening fire on groups of protestors, without drawing attention to himself.

Rabbi Jeremy Pearson was deeply affected by the sudden and violent death of his beloved wife Miriam. However, in addition to the overwhelming sense of loss, he felt personally responsible for what had happened. He could hardly blame little Shlomo although he had caused the car to lurch forward and provoked the trigger-happy soldier to open fire. It was up to him to protect his family and now his three young boys were motherless. Jeremy was a man of deep faith and he agonised on what he had done to cause God to punish him so severely.

The funeral occurred the day after the shooting. In Jewish law it is usual to bury all loved ones at the earliest possible time. This had become a problem in the chaotic dictatorship that Britain had become and Jeremy had often needed to intercede with the authorities to speed up the issue of death and committal certificates, for his congregants. Since the WDL had gained power, bureaucracy increased daily. Simple matters of everyday life became increasingly complicated. However, Jeremy had a new friend from an unlikely place. Captain Martin Benson was able to demand all the necessary certification and in Charleston's Britain no one argued with the army. Miriam was therefore buried in the Jewish cemetery just outside Gateshead in north eastern England where she had been born. He parents were deeply shocked as were all the members of her extended family.

Jeremy now had the huge problem of how to look after his children. At the end of the week of mourning his mother-in-law suggested that the three boys should stay with them. Jeremy was initially reluctant but realised this was probably the best solution, at least until he could get his own life back on track.

So one week after the terrible occurrence, Jeremy returned alone to Manchester to try to look after his congregation.

As if this had not been enough bad news he was told that one of his congregants had been arrested and accused of plotting against the government. This was a huge shock for Jeremy as this man, a close friend called Abe Jackson, was one of Jeremy's own group of fifteen. Now the Rabbi lived alone, without his family and he dreaded every knock on the door expecting that Abe would have admitted under torture to being a member of Jeremy's group and bent on 'treason,' as the authorities called it.

The year ended with a sad and lonely Jeremy wondering what further trials the Creator could have in store for him and what form these would take.

Chapter Twenty three

The loss of a friend

Colonel Sidney Charleston, the Prime Minister greeted the New Year with a sense of great achievement. He had set out to have one of the strongest democracies in the world reduced to being his personal fiefdom. The Royal family was still there in Buckingham Palace but after the execution of three minor royals for plotting against the 'democratic rights of the people,' they were just like every other household in the land; trying to stay alive by maintaining a low profile.

Parliament was suspended indefinitely under the 'state of emergency' now in its third year. Sidney ran the country from number 10 Downing street with the aid of a vast array of corrupt officials. Of his original group of fifteen only one survived; the Home Secretary, Angus Ferguson. He knew exactly how to retain his influential position. It was quite simple; all he had to do was to implement every instruction given to him by the Prime Minister, quickly and ruthlessly.

Sidney had often reflected on what an excellent move it had been to dispose with the services of the Chancellor of the Exchequer, Jacob Rothberg. Now he had ultimate control of the entire budget of the country. True, he reflected, government income was only a fraction of what it had been when he took power but he had been able to slash government spending by cancelling the National Health Service and substantially reducing the sums earmarked for education, welfare and other 'unnecessary' departments. As a result, after a secret and well-protected flight to Zurich, he had been able to open an account in a bank there and transfer billions of pounds. He had wondered if the senior bank authorities with whom he dealt, were at all suspicious of who he was, but he had quickly decided that his cover under the fictitious name of Reginald Cromby would be adequate protection. In any case, the account would only have a number and not a name. This was his first trip abroad since he had become Prime Minister and it was likely to be his only one. Now he had the account, all transactions could be undertaken electronically.

On a personal level Justine had originally proven to be an excellent wife. Socially, when entertaining she was graceful and every inch a lady. Daphne too had had those attributes and she had presented Sidney with two sons. However, in the bedroom there was no doubt which woman performed best; Justine.

As a generous gesture of gratitude for providing him with heirs, Charleston had decided to allow Daphne to stay on in Downing Street with her own suite of rooms. She deeply resented Justine but recognised that acquiescence would give her a comfortable life near her sons and she was well aware of what happened to people who did cross Sidney, such as her late lamented father. Deep within her heart she detested Sidney, both for what he had done to her and to her father and what he was doing to the country. However, she had far more determination and intelligence than Charleston gave her credit for and she bided her time.

In February Sidney threw a huge party to celebrate the birthday of his only remaining WDL cabinet member from the original group; one whose loyalty had always been without question. The Home Secretary was sixty years old and a glittering birthday dinner was organised for him. The evening had proceeded along traditional lines with a six course dinner, toasts to the birthday 'boy' and a musical entertainment. This consisted of a girl-band who, the Agency assured them, had played at many WDL functions. In addition, the girls did offer other services and these might be an advantage. The three scantily-clad girls sang and danced to the delight of the assembly and finished their presentation by inviting Angus to join them in a final number. They then, as the other guests departed, retired to accommodation that had been provided for them in Downing Street until the following day. Angus, who had been divorced years before, was known to be 'rather fond of the ladies,' as Sidney described this proclivity. Once all the other guests had left Sidney turned to Angus and whispered to him,

"Hang on. I have another surprise for you."

Sidney's two bodyguards were instructed to wait outside the door and would then accompany the PM to his private quarters after he left the banqueting suite.

The PM then turned to his wife Justine.

"Darling, you go on ahead. I have certain government matters to discuss with Angus. I will be up in less than half an hour," he promised

As soon as the coast was clear Sidney lifted a house phone and said,

"You can send them in now."

Within just a few moments the door of the now empty banqueting suite opened and in came the three girls who had provided the entertainment. Their previous attire had been fairly revealing and now they were covered up with belted raincoats.

Angus smiled.

"Are you young ladies going to sing again?"

All three girls answered him with smiles and the blonde girl in the middle proceeded to introduce them individually to the two men.

"This is Georgia, I am Candice and my other friend is Jessica."

Candice then stepped forward and pulled two dining chairs out onto the dance area facing where the girls stood.

"Gentlemen, please be seated and the show will begin."

Angus sat down next to Sidney who knew exactly what the new entertainment would involve. Suddenly, in unison, the three girls opened the belts of their raincoats. Underneath they were wearing the scantiest of underwear sets. They proceeded to sing as they allowed the coats to drop to the floor. Then they danced round the two men circling nearer and nearer until they touched them. Soon they were ruffling the hair of the two most powerful men in the country until Angus, with his powerful sex urge grabbed hold of Georgia and led her behind one of the tables where he finished unwrapping this birthday present!

Sidney knew his wife Justine would be waiting for him and he told the other two girls to stay with Angus and see what further service they could be to him, after Georgia had finished.

What Sidney did not know was that the girl who called herself Georgia was the young widow of a 'dissident' who had 'unfortunately' died while in custody. She was already a member of a fifteen group and was prepared to make any sacrifice necessary to destroy Angus who she knew was personally responsible for her loss. The other two girls were members of her fifteen.

On the morning after the party, the cleaners discovered the naked and mutilated body of the Home Secretary in the room where he had celebrated his last ever birthday.

Sidney was furious. He had lost the one and only man who had always given him total unswerving loyalty. He was determined to exact swift retribution on whoever had provided the girls but all attempts to trace the agency proved futile.

Sidney himself went on radio and television to announce the 'tragic' death of the Home Secretary from a heart attack and spoke warmly and genuinely of his only true friend. It occurred to him that he himself could have been the target. He knew that he was almost certainly the most hated man in Britain and probably in Europe. However, he had always wanted to control the country and he was enough of a realist to recognise that to exercise the power he now had over the lives (and deaths) of millions of people, would hardly make him popular.

Chapter twenty four

Family Affairs

Sidney had two sons by his first wife Daphne. They were Edgar and Charles. They both held commissions in the army and although their father was proud of this he still secretly considered them to be wimps as they completely lacked his ruthless determination. However, after the assassination of Angus, Sidney realised that steps must be taken to improve security for all the family. He therefore arranged for the two young men, now thirty and twenty five respectively, to be transferred from army houses in the north of England to office jobs in the Ministry of Defence in London. Charles was still unmarried and appeared to be wedded to his career while Edgar had been wed to Tricia for two years now and had already produced a son.

Sidney had always favoured his elder offspring anyway and now that Edgar had made him a grandfather, he was installed in a self-contained apartment in number 11 Downing street where Sidney felt they would be safe.

It has to be said that once the family was living next door, Sidney began to visit frequently, ostensibly to see his baby grandson, Julian. However, it must also be stated that he was very impressed with his daughter-in-law, and she with him.

Tricia was stunning. She was very tall, almost six feet and had copper-toned hair that cascaded down to her shoulders. Her figure was classical and she carried herself as a woman of such statuesque proportions should.

Sidney was by now beginning to tire of Justine. She was still as adventurous as ever in bed but as his power had grown so had her ambition, especially for her elderly parents. Since the WDL had become the government, Charleston had discontinued the time-honoured practice of granting honours. It was of course not really for him to bestow them anyway, but the Royal family, in the old days when Britain had been a constitutional monarchy, had granted these honours at the recommendation of the then government. Sidney, however, wanted nothing to do with the Royal family and as long as they stayed out of the public eye, he was content to leave them languishing in Buckingham Palace.

Now he had his second wife frequently suggesting that her father should be given a peerage.

"Look Justine," he repeatedly told her, "I want nothing to do with peers and peerages, knights and all that other rubbish. They are a symbol of our royalist past."

But Justine would not let the matter rest and in the end it led to a full-blown row.

For a man with the power of life and death over millions of people, what was the life of one young woman more or less? She had served him well enough at first but had not even produced a child. At least Daphne had two sons to her credit and now a grandson had been produced. Sidney resolved that Justine would have to go.

A second divorce would be too complicated, he reasoned, somewhat inconsistently. Anyway, he decided, the way Justine was pressurising him, divorce would be too good for her. However there were always other ways. A senior policeman in the Metropolitan force, a man deeply grateful to Sidney for his promotion to Chief Superintendent, was told that the Prime Minister wished to consult him on a private matter. He arrived punctually and was taken to Sidney's private office.

David Ingram was a university graduate who, impatient with the lack of financial rewards from his career in a large solicitors' office, eventually used moneys from the firm's client account to purchase an expensive car to impress his girl-friend. This was back in 2010 and after his crime was discovered he had been tried and sentenced to a period in prison. As the judge expressed himself,

"If the legal officers of the country are not to be trusted, then we really have nothing left."

He languished there until the late unlamented Home Secretary, Angus Ferguson, was searching for men who could be drafted into the new police force and would be essential in maintaining the WDL style of law and order. Ferguson quickly discovered Ingram's file and with a background in the law, he was ideal material. Ingram was thus released and found himself provided with a well paid job as a Police Inspector, all on the same day.

The Prime Minister was behind his desk and rose to greet the now Chief Superintendent Ingram with the charm he could always muster to meet the occasion.

"Ah," Sidney began, with a broad smile. "My dear Chief Superintendent; it is good to see you again. Please be seated. There is something I wish to discuss with you."

David Ingram had been more than a little worried after the summons to attend on the Prime Minister had arrived. He had met Charleston before but any dealings with the WDL government had always been through Angus and the Home Secretary was now dead. Surely, he pondered, the PM is not taking on that portfolio as well as Foreign affairs and the Exchequer? Then why had been sent for by the head of government; a man he knew to be utterly ruthless? However, the warmth of the welcome reassured him and he waited patiently for Sidney to get to the point.

Firstly, however, Sidney enquired about Robert's career and casually mentioned that he would probably be in line when the next commissioner of the Met was appointed.

Then Charleston got down to business.

"Please understand that this matter is totally confidential. Not a word of the conversation, we are about to have, can be repeated outside this room. That includes your boss the Commissioner and your wife and family."

David expressed horror at the very suggestion that he would ever leak a conversation with the Prime Minister to a living soul. Was he not a totally trustworthy person; a senior police officer? Apart from the long forgotten dipping expedition into the client account years ago, he considered himself an important pillar in the maintenance of law and order in WDL Britain.

"Of course not, Sir," he replied to the PM. "I think you must know I am the soul of discretion and completely trustworthy."

"Yes, of course," Sidney replied quickly. The last thing he wanted was appear to question the integrity of someone from whom he was about to demand a very special and delicate service.

"I suspect my wife is being unfaithful to me," he began with a feigned expression of distress on his face.

"I think she must be a nymphomaniac as from what I can gather, she has been seeing at least three men simultaneously."

There was, of course, not one shred of evidence to support this allegation but Sidney had to justify the course of events he was about to propose not only to David but also to himself. Self-delusion had long been one of Sidney's strongest points. This great attribute had long-ago destroyed any conscience that he may once have had.

"Putting it to you bluntly, my dear Robert," he said. "I can speak to you bluntly, can't I, Robert?"

David nodded gravely, wondering what the PM was about to suggest.

"A divorce would not be an appropriate remedy for someone in my position." He chose to forget that less than three years ago he had divorced Daphne.

"I need you to find an attractive young gentleman with a violent streak. Someone you suspect may be raping and murdering women. If you can find such a person and I am sure that it will not be too difficult, we will simply have to arrange an introduction."

David nodded again. He knew that there were many such men at large in the London. They hardly warranted serious police attention as anything that terrorised the population, kept them even more cowed and afraid than they already were, was very useful.

"It is important that this man should be well-educated and good looking as otherwise Justine will simply avoid him. Once you have a likely person, I will arrange for them to meet at an appropriate venue," the Prime Minister explained. "Please let me know as soon as you have a candidate."

And so the fate of Justine, secretary, mistress and finally wife to Colonel Sidney Charleston was sealed, or so it seemed.

Chapter twenty five

Reluctant Acquiescence

Rabbi Jeremy Pearson was a sad man. His wife was dead and his young children were living with his in-laws, one hundred and forty five miles away up in the north east of England. With the government-imposed restrictions on travel and his responsibilities to his congregants, he had only seen them once since the tragic accident that had deprived him of a wife, and them of a mother.

It was a bright, sunny evening in early summer and Jeremy was studying a tractate of the Talmud at his desk. It was well before the curfew hour of 9.00pm and a ring on the door-bell occasioned no surprise. His congregants often visited him to obtain his advice on religious and personal matters. He placed a book mark in the page he had been reading, closed the large, leather-bound volume and stepped out into the hall to open the door. However, it was not a congregant to consult him but a man he had not seen for some months; Andrew Robertson. This was a surprise and a pleasant one for Jeremy. It had worried him that his refusal of Andrew's request to impersonate the Prime Minister had disappointed his new friend and he knew that Andrew was a good man who was frequently placing himself in danger for the good of other people. However, he was also convinced that he, Jeremy, was not really the right man to impersonate Sidney Charleston and that decision had only been confirmed by recent events.

Andrew had been conspicuously absent since the refusal and it was now well over six months since the groups of fifteen had been organised.

"Hello Andrew, well this is a nice surprise. I have often wondered what had happened to you," Jeremy greeted him.

They sat facing each other across Jeremy's desk. Andrew looked very serious.

"Rabbi, firstly may I offer you my heartfelt condolences. You don't need to tell me the dreadful story of what happened to your wife. I was told soon afterwards by someone who was there."

Jeremy looked at him in amazement.

"By someone who was there?" he queried.

"Yes," replied Andrew. "A very good friend of mine, Captain Martin Benson."

"Oh, so you know the officer?" Jeremy enquired, his thoughts going back again to that terrible morning on the moors.

"I certainly do and he is one of our contacts inside the military trying to do his best to stop the trigger-happy yobs in uniform from doing to other people what they did to your poor lady."

"He was certainly very kind to me and enabled me to have my wife buried the following day, in accordance with our customs," Jeremy explained. "I will never forget his kindness and coming from a man who wears the hated uniform that is now so much associated with oppression, it was all the more wonderful."

"Can I now ask you if there have been any repercussions for your group of fifteen?" Jeremy enquired, completely changing the subject.

Jeremy nodded.

"A very nice man called Abe Jackson, one of my congregants was arrested and charged with plotting against the government. It is a few weeks ago now and there have been no further repercussions, so I hope and pray that he has been able to avoid naming anyone else."

Andrew now used his own private code to write anything incriminating into his pocket note-book.

"Abe Jackson," he said as he wrote something that looked entirely different.

"Any other problems that I should know about?" Andrew enquired.

"Well, there is something else I would like to discus with you," the Rabbi answered.

"I have felt very guilty for turning you down when you asked me to impersonate Charleston. I still do not believe I could do this but, if you wish, I can at least hear what your plan was, rather than dismissing it out of hand."

"That is the main reason I am here," Andrew explained. "I hoped you might have given the matter more thought."

Andrew then explained that Jeremy would be dressed in the colonel's uniform that the PM often wore.

"Possibly the most difficult thing for you would be shaving off of your beard?" he suggested.

"Yes and that was the first thing I thought of when you tried to broach the subject before. There are a number of Rabbis who do not have beards; it is not essential; maybe preferable but not essential! However there are two problems associated with being clean-shaven. Firstly, from what I can see Charleston has such a close resemblance that people would think I was he, when I wasn't deliberately impersonating him. Also," he continued, "my own congregation would find it strange to see me clean shaven."

"That really is easily solved," Andrew explained. "We have a young man in our organisation who was a TV make-up artist in the days when TV drama was allowed. He would make you a false beard that replicated exactly the real beard you now have."

Jeremy nodded rather unenthusiastically and said,

"So what is the rest of the plan?"

Andrew then outlined all the details of what would be required of Jeremy. This took about an hour during which time Jeremy's reactions, as shown by his facial expressions, went from horror to indignation and from fear to respect for whoever could have thought up such a plan.

When Andrew had finished they both sat back in their chairs and issued an almost simultaneous sigh. Andrew's was from the sheer exhaustion of talking with so much concentration and for so long whereas the Rabbi was both terrified of the plan and at the same time sorely tempted to say yes to it.

Andrew now sat quietly watching Jeremy as he agonised over where his greater duty lay. He then asked Andrew to excuse him while he went into another room to pray for God's guidance in making the right decision.

However, other matters were afoot that were to seriously affect both Jeremy's decision and the original plan.

CHAPTER TWENTY SIX

ROGER & OUT!

Roger Iveson was in his thirties and had been a man in serious pursuit of artificially induced happiness ever since he had left university under a heavy black cloud, as a result of trying to sell cocaine to fellow undergraduates. His father had been a night-club owner whose main income came from introducing innocent young men to young ladies of doubtful virtue. The Ivesons, however, were a 'fine' old family who claimed to be able to trace their ancestry back to the Norman invasion in 1066. How they had sunk to the decadent levels of Roger et Pere, was hard to understand? However, sink, they had. They were rotten to the core.

In 2008 Iveson Senior was stabbed to death by a Russian tourist whose anger at being robbed by the gentleman in question, drove him into an incontrollable rage. Roger, after a few days of mourning for his father and mentor, took over the family business and proceeded to make a very satisfactory income out of the proceeds of high-class pimping and drug dealing.

Roger spoke with the upper-class drawl that more respectable members of the aristocracy had become anxious to lose. He dressed in Savile Row suits and only the best casual clothes, as worn by the country set. He was tall and slim with an inherited shock of blonde hair that was credited to his Norman/Norsemen ancestors.

In 2010 Roger decided to purchase a country house with his ill-gotten gains. This was at a time when the economies of most western countries, including Britain were showing signs of irreversible collapse.

He had never married and cared not at all for the fact that he would be the last of the Ivesons. He installed three of his women in the house to attend to his creature comforts, and satisfy his voracious sexual appetite. The 2010 general election had no effect whatsoever on his income and activities and he continued to amass large sums of money until the collapse of the Provincial Bank in 2013. This was the first time that the British government had allowed a bank to go under and to take so many investors with it but the government itself, like all the governments in Western Europe, was in deep trouble after the collapse of the Euro.

Roger was furious but his money was lost and he had to face the situation. He mortgaged his beautiful home in Hertfordshire and resolved to never again invest his money in one bank. However; much worse was to follow.

In 2015 the WDL became the government and immediately set to work in closing down most of the British leisure industry. As soon as Charleston had decreed a state of emergency, all forms of public entertainment were banned. Roger's nightclub, which was the 'front' for all his other and illegal activities, was closed.

Once again Roger was furious and impotent to do anything to reverse the disastrous turn that his fortunes had now taken. His impotence was also manifested in the bedroom and not one of the young ladies could obtain even a glimmer of interest from him on their visits to his bed. Roger thus became angrier and angrier and increasingly frustrated and started to take out his fury on the unfortunate young women.

"You are bloody useless," he would bellow at them.

"It is because you have turned into such an ugly old bag that I don't fancy you any more," he told Valerie who had hitherto been his favourite.

Then one night his anger got the better of him and he battered the unfortunate girl into senselessness. He had hitherto been unaware of his psychotic tendencies but achieved in violence and murder the satisfaction denied to him by normal relationships. He buried the girl in his large and now overgrown garden and told her two 'house-mates' that he had sent her home. The following night he invited both the remaining young women into his bedroom for a 'threesome' and, in a frenzy he dealt with them in a similar manner to their late friend.

The house was put on the market. There were, of course no buyers for country houses in Charleston's Britain and once all his other assets had been sold, at break down prices, he was forced to take the train to London to discuss the situation with the bank that now held the deeds to his property. This bank, the Royal Commercial, was one of the few financial institutions that continued to function due to it being the bank used by the Prime Minister and his friends for transmitting monies to his Swiss account. The manager, Tony Arbuthnot, was a close friend of Charleston and told Roger that he had just one calendar month to bring the account up to date. Otherwise the bank would foreclose. Two months later Roger Iveson was destitute and homeless.

Then the thing he most dreaded occurred. The bank decided to use his old home as a training centre and set about making the necessary changes and alterations to the property. The rear garden was to become a car park and it was then that the corpses of the three unfortunate women were discovered. The police were called and a warrant was issued for Roger's arrest.

Roger Iveson now lived in London in a cardboard box under a railway bridge. All attempts to find him were to no avail. In any case the Met had far more important tasks to undertake in arresting and incarcerating dissidents. The murder of three young women was a fairly minor crime when compared with the serious charges of treason against the government of Colonel Sidney Charleston.

Once settled into his new cardboard residence Roger set about obtaining sexual satisfaction in the only way he now could, by murdering young women. Most of his victims were prostitutes, living on the streets as he and countless other Londoners now did. It took some four years before a policeman caught Roger in the act of dismembering the body of a poor girl under a disused railway bridge. He was arrested and locked up in Wormwood Scrubs without the luxury of a trial. He was about to be arbitrarily executed when his case came to the notice of Chief Superintendent David Ingram.

It was one of David Ingram's tasks to authorise all executions of the poor miscreants who had not had the luxury of a trial; fair or otherwise. David knew the name Roger Iveson as he recalled a man with that name at university. If this was the Roger Iveson he remembered, judging by both his crimes and previous background, he would be the ideal candidate to undertake the delicate task of disposing of his friend the Prime Minister's wife, Justine.

So, Roger was released, showered and shaved, supplied with elegant brand-new and obviously expensive casual clothing and escorted to a meeting with the second most powerful policeman in London.

Roger was mystified. Why take so much trouble with the appearance of a man about to be given a lethal injection to terminate his life?

David Ingram had thought long and hard about how he would broach the subject of the PMs wife with Roger. After due consideration he decided to let nature, that is Roger's violent nature, take its course.

A lavish dinner party was arranged for the 'great and (not so) good' who were Charleston's close friends and confederates. Much to Roger's astonishment he was told by David Ingram that, as compensation for the way he had been treated, he was to accompany David to the event. Roger, however, was intelligent enough to realise that when other murderers and sundry criminals were suddenly released from prison, this was to carry out some service for the regime.

"Does this mean that I am pardoned?" he enquired.

"Yes, of course," David replied, "once you have attended the party, you will be a free man."

Roger was astonished. He had attended many parties in his time, mostly somewhat wild events in country homes. Now, all that was apparently expected of him was to attend a celebration and by doing so, secure his release from jail. He could hardly believe his good fortune.

Everybody who was anybody was invited and the first to arrive to welcome the guests, was Sidney Charleston accompanied by his 'deeply cherished' wife.

David and Roger were early arrivals and mingled with the other guests. Roger, of course was well accustomed to attending events of this nature before he had lost all his money. This was the world he knew and he set about charming the men and women present with his personality. Most of the women, however, were middle-aged and although mainly well-groomed and attractive were well over Roger's preferred age of thirty something. The woman who really attracted him was out of reach, or so he thought.

Justine, the Prime Minister's wife, was wearing a red chiffon gown with a plunging neckline and the back cut away in a manner that left little to the imagination.

Half way through dinner the prime minister announced that he had been called away on urgent state business and Justine was furious. She started to look around the room at the other male guests and tall blond handsome Roger stood out from the crowd. Why had she never seen him before? She wondered.

Roger had watched Sidney Charleston depart and wondered whether he might approach Justine for a dance. He asked Robert's opinion and he, much to

Roger's amazement, saw no reason why he should not introduce himself.

Justine, in the meantime, had walked over to the bar. She knew that the eyes of every male at the gathering would be on her as she strode across the room. She was well aware that she was married to the most powerful man in the country; a man who held the lives and deaths of the entire population within his grasp. However, she considered herself to be in an incredibly strong position. It was only three years since he had divorced his previous wife and Justine's own prowess in the bedroom, she considered was more than enough to ensure Sidney's enduring love and loyalty. The prime minister would never divorce her. She was certain of that.

She settled herself on a bar stool and ordered her usual tipple of Vodka and orange. At that moment she became conscious of someone standing too close to her to be accidental when the rest of the bar area was deserted. She glanced round to ascertain who was invading her space and saw that it was the tall blond man who she had been secretly watching during most of the evening. She was relieved and delighted. The relief was that the man was not one of the minders usually appointed by her husband to protect her and attend to her wishes. The delight was that here, standing next to her, was this handsome, aristocratic looking man who she really fancied.

"Hello," he began, with a smile that would have melted far less receptive hearts than hers. "You look so lonely here; may I join you for a drink and a chat?"

"Do you know who I am?" she countered.

"Of course," the man replied. "The whole country knows that the Prime Minister is blessed with the most beautiful and charming lady in the land."

"In that case," she answered, taking the compliment without demur. "Please draw up a stool and by all means let us converse."

In view of the fact that that the pair had separately spent most of the evening longing to meet, the conversation flowed seamlessly.

Roger was obliged to provide personal information to satisfy the enquiries of the lady and told her in some detail of his life and extraction. Not surprisingly he failed to mention his drug-trading and pimping activities and the fact that he had been awaiting a date for his execution on the charge of murder of three young women who had been his unwilling guests in his country house.

Eventually he decided that Justine would now be sufficiently impressed with him to accept an invitation to dance and in fact he longed to run his hand over her delicious naked back.

They danced away the rest of the evening.

Justine had decided that Sidney had no right to leave early and thus neglect her and if anyone reported her behaviour with this charming gentleman, she would soon make it clear that she had needed a companion to help pass the time at this tedious dinner party, after her husband had deserted her.

Roger, for his part, had suddenly re-discovered his sexual drive with this beautiful woman in his arms after his impotence with his previous and now deceased girl-friends. He cared little for the consequences as he felt he was already on borrowed time, a fact that puzzled him not a little. By midnight most of the other guests had departed and only his 'minder' David and a few other people remained.

Roger and Justine were now the only couple still dancing and as the evening had progressed she had moulded her beautiful figure closer and closer to his as they both became aware of the urgency of their desire for each other. By the end of the evening he had resolved to try to arrange a further meeting with this exciting woman where matters could be taken to their natural conclusion. However, should she be a willing party to such an assignation, he agonised on whether he would still be alive to keep the date? The Chief Superintendent had told him he would be free to leave after the party but he could hardly forget that he had been under sentence of death when he was suddenly catapulted from the depths of despair to this glittering function.

Eventually Roger whispered into her ear,
"When can I see you again?"
To his amazement she stopped dancing and led him by the hand out of the banqueting suite. As he left he glanced to where Robert was sitting and was amazed to see this senior member of the Metropolitan police signalling his approval with a 'thumbs up' sign.

Justine had her own quarters within the building and the pair made their way silently to a doorway at the end of a long corridor. She opened the door, still clutching his hand and as soon as the door closed again she turned to face Roger and planted a long lingering kiss on his lips.

She then led him to an inner bedroom where her dress mysteriously slithered to the floor around her ankles. It took only another minute for the pair to be locked in a passionate embrace on top of the gleaming white satin sheets. Roger forgot all his previous sexual inadequacy and they spent the night together in a series of highly successful couplings.

It was six o'clock in the morning when Justine awoke the slumbering Roger and told him he must leave.

"I always have breakfast with my husband at eight o'clock," she explained and in the sober light of dawn she had suddenly realised that the anger of the most powerful man in the country could be very dangerous for her health and that of her new lover.

Roger dressed quickly and bade his farewells. David had supplied him with £200 'pocket money' and he decided to find a coffee shop, have breakfast and then telephone David at a more sociable hour.

At eight o'clock that morning there were two deeply shocked men in London and one of them was in a state of uncontrollable anger with the other.

Justine now dressed primly in a tailored suit entered the quarters of her husband Sidney Charleston for breakfast. She was initially greeted by the facial expression of someone who thought he was seeing a ghost. Sidney Charleston however, had not survived a military career and then hijacked an entire country by being phased for very long by the obvious, if unexpected survival of one woman.

"Hello, my dear," he greeted her, after a momentary pause. "Do join me for breakfast."

Sidney was, of course seething with anger and once his wife was settled at the table he excused himself to make an important telephone call. In the next room and comfortably out the earshot of his wife he telephoned the Chief Commissioner of the Metropolitan Police and ordered the immediate arrest of his erstwhile 'friend' David Ingram.

In the meantime, David had been shocked to receive a phone call from Roger. He concluded that if the latter would have murdered the Prime Minister's wife as planned; he would hardly have expected to hear from him again. Somehow, Justine Charleston had tamed this vicious killer. It was at this juncture that the door to his office was flung open and he himself was placed under arrest by two of his colleagues working on the instructions of the Chief Commissioner. The charge was of course, Treason.

Neither, Justine nor Roger had the slightest idea that they had thwarted a plan to bring about her untimely death and they resolved to continue their liaison at the first possible opportunity.

Later that day Roger tried once again to contact David Ingram and was horrified to discover that the man who had granted him a new lease of life was now in prison. He decided that if he was now to survive he must return to his recent existence among the dregs of society.

As for Justine, she had a totally different and non-sexual agenda. She had to admit to herself that Roger was a satisfying lover and that was one reason for wanting to meet up with him again. However, when she was unable to contact him again she focussed her attention on other matters. She was just one of millions of people who wished the Prime Minister anything but good health.

CHAPTER TWENTY SEVEN

TRICIA

The Prime Minister's obsession with his daughter-in-law continued to grow and it soon became apparent to him that she, in turn, appeared to be more than a little impressed with him. He decided, therefore to send his son Edgar off to the north for a month to deal with civil disturbance in Newcastle-on-Tyne.

"Don't worry, my boy," Sidney assured him. "I will personally make sure that your wife and son want for nothing while you are away."

And he was as good as his word. He sincerely doted on his little grandson who seemed, even at this tender age, to have inherited Sidney's obsessive determination to have his own way. The Prime Minister's sons had been a great disappointment to him and now all his hopes for a dynastic future for the Charleston's were vested in this little boy.

As for Edgar's wife, Tricia, Sidney would certainly ensure that she wanted for nothing. As soon as Edgar was safely installed in the north east, Sidney started visiting her most evenings.

Once his attempt to permanently dispose of his wife Justine had failed, he decided to use her public behaviour with Roger Iveson as a weapon.

"Your behaviour that night was unforgivable. Did you not think I would be told about the disgusting way you threw yourself at that man? I am going to divorce you but only when I am good and ready. In the meantime you may stay here but, other than sex, I want nothing to do with you."

Apart from the 'sex' pronouncement, this was good news to her. She had hated Sidney for some time now and had only married him to fulfil her own long term agenda. The less she saw of him the better!

Tricia Charleston, the Prime Minister's daughter-in-law had been excluded from school at the age of fifteen for dealing in drugs. She had never been known to take them herself, but the toll of impressionable boys and girls who she had tempted down this disastrous path had already reached epidemic proportions when she was discovered. She had also made it her personal mission, from the tender age of thirteen, to personally destroy the virginity of most of the boys in the school as soon as they arrived at puberty. This she did as a favour to them and as one good turn deserved another, she always accepted gratefully the gifts they 'forced' upon her to show their gratitude.

Her 'loving' parents insisted that she left their home once her school activities were discovered. Although they were hardly pillars of the community themselves, they certainly could not have been expected to continue to provide a home for such a daughter. Fortunately, as may be gathered, she was wordly wise and had the appearance of an eighteen year old. She was tall and possessed of a fine full figure that drew admiring glances from virtually every male who saw her.

Tricia did not believe in wasting time and on the day she departed from the shelter of the family she found accommodation and a job as a lap-dancer. For the next three years she concentrated on her career and was able to accumulate a healthy bank balance. Apart from the physical activity she indulged in to achieve this, her cash-flow was enhanced by supplying a number of the other and weaker minded girls with drugs.

At the age of eighteen she purchased her first property and, after converting it into a number of one room flats, she let these, mainly to other girls where they could entertain their gentlemen friends. She now resigned from her career as a lap-dancer and concentrated on expanding her property empire. As a result, when Edgar met her one night, some three years later, in a queue for the cinema, she was already affecting the accent and dress of the upper classes.

She told him a romanticised and somewhat less than truthful account of how her education had been tragically cut short as a result of the 'untimely death of her parents.' How she had used the money they left her to build up a portfolio of properties. Edgar, now an army officer but hardly the brightest in his year at Sandhurst, was very impressed. After a whirlwind romance and with the backing of his parents they were married.

The wedding of Tricia & Edgar took place in the year when the WDL assumed power and, if the truth be known, Tricia was far more impressed by her father-in-law than by her husband. Poor Edgar was just a stepping stone in her ultimate ambition to become the consort of the most powerful man in the land. Tricia knew, as did the entire government and civil service, that Justine's days were numbered. *What kind of idiot goes playing around when married to the Prime Minister?* Of course, both she and her quarry could sense the strong attraction they had for each other. She knew precisely why Edgar had been sent away and on Sidney's second nocturnal visit after his son had been posted to Newcastle, it was no surprise for them to find themselves engaging in passionate if violent sex in her matrimonial boudoir.

Colonel Sidney Charleston was a man of voracious appetites. The first of these was for power and this had been achieved. Now the task was to hold on to it. Then there was his appetite for sex. He still continued to 'use' Justine although he despised her for her disloyalty in making a public spectacle with Roger. *A man has his needs,* he would whisper to himself. Now he had the services of an additional woman and one who he actually liked and admired. She had guts and determination and he liked that, providing it was only used in his favour. Finally there was his appetite for food. He devoured his food quickly and in large quantities. Amazingly, he never put on weight. This was probably because the excessive sexual activity burned up the calories provided by the huge platefuls he devoured.

As soon as he discovered how well Tricia and he performed together in bed he arranged for his son Edgar's posting to the north east of England to be extended for a further twelve months. He emailed to tell the poor unsuspecting fellow how proud he was of him and not to worry about his wife and son. Everything was fine.

However, little by little Sidney Charleston's paradise and everyone else's hell was about to slowly unravel and this started from a most unlikely source.

Chapter Twenty eight

Just good friends

Captain Edgar Charleston adored his wife and telephoned every evening from the flat the army provided for him in Newcastle. She, at first, professed undying love for him and they both bemoaned the necessity to be apart from each other for so long.

His brother Charles, unmarried although secretly involved in a homosexual relationship with one James Benson, met his beloved in the latter's flat in Mayfair at least three times each week. Charles, of course, had no idea that James had a brother in the army by the name of Martin. Nor was he to know that both Martin and James were involved in the secret opposition and along with Andrew Robertson were founders of the first group of fifteen. Indeed it was fortunate that James was gay as that had made his first meeting far easier to arrange.

After the WDL had closed down all clubs, heterosexual or gay, groups of gays in London had taken to meeting in each others homes. James was a frequent visitor to two or three of these groups and after discovering that Charles Charleston was an occasional visitor to one of them, he discussed how they could use the sexual orientation of the Prime Minister's younger son to advantage. Martin Benson had long since accepted that his brother was gay and they remained firm friends after he 'came out' at the age of twenty one. Now the brothers were in their thirties, lived their own lives but were both resolved to work towards the freeing of the country from the yoke of the tyranny of the WDL dictatorship of Sidney Charleston.

In consultation with Andrew Robertson it had been decided that James should befriend the Prime Minister's younger son Charles. This proved to be easily achieved and in fact James genuinely liked Charles.

Charles spent his days at his desk in the Ministry of Defence and returned each evening to his quarters in Downing Street. Then on Mondays, Wednesdays and Fridays he would repair after an early dinner to the flat of his special friend James. He would stay there all night as the curfew imposed by his father's government meant he could not return to his own Downing Street quarters until 6 o'clock the following morning.

Sidney had no idea that his younger son was gay. Despite his own active life style he did however notice Charles frequent absences and presumed that Charles must be involved with a girl friend. His regular nights out left, in his mind, no other possible explanation. The alternative, that his son might be gay, never occurred to him. It was unthinkable for Sidney, the tough unscrupulous soldier who now ruled Britain with an iron fist, that a member of the Charleston family could be anything but 'straight.' However, he began to wonder why Charles never brought a girl friend home. His son was obviously in a long term relationship and he needed to make sure that the 'young lady' he was seeing was suitable. So Sidney arranged to have Charles followed. He instructed a promising young sergeant, Craig Thompson, from the Metropolitan police to shadow Charles and report back directly to Sidney. The report, when it came was deeply shocking to the Prime Minister.

"Sir," Craig told the PM, sitting opposite him in the latter's private office. "This is somewhat embarrassing. Your son Charles is a regular overnight visitor to the flat of a man called James Benson."

"Oh, I see," Sidney replied. "And does this man Benson have a daughter?"

"No Sir," Craig continued. "He is a man in his thirties and he is a known homosexual."

The Prime Minister exploded. "How dare you! Are you insinuating that my son is gay?"

Craig held his ground although he knew he was now in deep trouble himself. *What kind of a career could there be for a man who knew the Prime Minister's son was gay.* This reaction was exactly what he feared when given the errand. When he discovered the identity of Charles Charlesworth's 'friend' he had been tempted to lie to the PM but decided that this could land him in even more trouble when the deceit was discovered. How wrong he was!

"Sir," Craig continued bravely, "you asked who Charles was visiting so regularly and I have told you the facts. How you interpret them is up to you."

"Just a minute," Sidney barked in a voice choked with anger. He rose from his desk leaving the unfortunate police sergeant sitting there and made his way into an adjoining room.

Once the door was firmly closed he sat heavily in an armchair to consider the thunderbolt that Craig had just delivered. He would send for his son and challenge him with this information. First, however, he must deal with this 'upstart' policeman. He lifted the phone and demanded the immediate presence of four of his personal bodyguards, men selected from the ranks of violent criminals.

As soon as the men arrived they were told,

"There is a man sitting at my desk in the next room who is guilty of treason. However, I do not want him to be taken to prison. You can escort him downstairs and into the cellar and there you can dispose of him on the basis that he tried to escape from your custody. Do I make myself clear?"

The men nodded.

"However, before he even leaves this room I want him gagged. On no account may any of you have any conversation with him."

That sadly was the end of the promising career and life of Sergeant Craig Thompson.

Once the men had departed the Prime Minister lifted the telephone again. This time it was to telephone the Ministry of Defence.

"I need to speak to Captain Charles Charleston," he demanded.

"Who is this calling?" the young woman who had answered the phone enquired.

"This is his father, the Prime Minister," Sidney answered in a voice like thunder.

A split second later Charles voice came over the phone.

Sidney knew he needed to approach his son gently and casually. He tried to sound pleasant.

"Hello, my boy!" he said. "There is something I would like to talk over with you. How soon could you get here."

"Father," Charles replied. "I will come at once." He knew better than to keep his father waiting even if it was only for a chat. "I will just tell my C.O. that you want to see me and I should be back in Downing Street within half an hour."

Once again Sidney sat back in his armchair to consider how he would approach this delicate matter with his younger son. Normally he was a man who made instant decisions but this was family and therefore different. He was furious and deeply outraged.

Twenty five minutes later Charles was ushered into his father's office. He thought he had been summoned to discuss some military matter. Had his brother not been despatched to the north to deal with an insurrection there? However, one look at his father's face disabused him of that idea. He had known from childhood by the way his father glared and stared when he was in trouble, and he knew something serious was afoot.

"Sit down, Charles," Sidney bellowed. "Now who the hell is James Benson?"

"A friend of mine, sir," Charles answered, shaking with terror.

"Really," Sidney answered in a voice full of irony. "A friend. How nice. And what do you get up to with this friend three times a week?" he demanded.

"Sir," Charles again replied. "He is just a good friend."

"Don't you mean a homosexual lover?" the older man demanded, his voice rising in indignation.

Charles knew that when Sidney was building up the WDL he always spoke about how inclusive the party would be. It was to include all races in the United Kingdom and all minority groups such as homosexuals and lesbians. However, he also knew that Sidney despised and detested anyone who was not heterosexual. Once he had assumed power he had purged all the people who did not conform to his idea of normality from the government and all its agencies.

"You need not reply," Sidney bellowed. "It is only too clear to me what has been going on. You will never see this pervert again. You can go to work in the Ministry each day but I expect you home for dinner each night and after that you are grounded. "No more disgusting little outings to see your lover. Do you understand?"

"Yes sir," Charles answered trembling.

After a momentary pause Sidney continued, "In a few days time you will be posted to a garrison well away from London and your senior officers will be told to keep you on a tight rein. Is that clear? You may be my son but I will not put up with your deviant behaviour any longer. I am sure you know that nasty things can happen to people who cross me. Don't ever do that or I may forget our relationship and deal with you as you really deserve."

"Now get out of here," Sidney finished.

Charles rose from the chair in which he had been sitting, visibly shaking and made his way out of the room.

He started to walk back towards the ministry where he worked and realised that he had now placed the life of his friend James in serious danger. He must warn him. But how?

Chapter Twenty nine

The Curfew Breaker

It was eleven o'clock on a warm summer evening and Andrew Robertson was quietly making his way through the deserted streets of north Manchester towards the house of his friend Rabbi Jeremy Pearson. At that time of the year the sun sank late and anyone foolhardy enough to wish to break the curfew could not start his journey before ten thirty. Andrew had his own technique of travelling during the curfew nights and that involved many miles of nocturnal walking. He wore trainers to ensure his footsteps would not be detected and he stayed in the shadows keeping as near as possible to the walls of buildings and away from the occasional street lights that were still allowed to be illuminated in WDL Britain. He was coming from his home in Worsley and had trod these paths many times over the last two or three years. The greatest danger was always crossing major roads as this was where the police and army curfew enforcement groups would be stationed. The most worrying place for him was near the Agecroft Power Station where he was forced to cross the road. He had however, crossed at what he considered the safest point, many times before but on this occasion his luck ran out. He was halfway across the road when a searchlight ream forced him to stop in his tracks.

"Where do you think you are going?" boomed a voice over a loudspeaker.

Within seconds he was surrounded by six armed soldiers all pointing their guns at him menacingly. Andrew stood still wondering what would happen next until an army officer strode up to him.

"What is your name and why are you out during the curfew?" the officer demanded.

"My name is Jonathan Mackintosh and my child is ill so I am on my way to the doctors," he lied.

"I need to see your ID papers," the officer replied.

Andrew patted his pockets and then searched each one knowing full well that they were all empty.

"Sorry, Officer," he eventually said. "I was so worried about my little boy that I have come out without them."

"I am equally sorry Mr Mackintosh, if that is what your name is, but you are under arrest. Curfew breaking and failing to supply ID papers are both serious offences and could land you with a prison sentence of at least five years. Men!" he called to his troops. "Take him away!"

With that the officer turned on his heel and rough hands grabbed Andrew and pushed him in to the back of an army van.

However, as he climbed in he glanced back at the soldiers and realised that another officer had joined the group of men standing in the dimly lit street. Then he recognised the newcomer. It was his friend and co-conspirator Major Martin Benson. He looked right at Andrew and nodded.

"What is his name?" he demanded in a voice loud enough for Andrew to hear.

The other officer answered,

"He says his name is Jonathan Mackintosh."

Martin gave a curt nod and added,

"I am sick and tired of these curfew breakers. Get him off to prison. That will teach him to obey the law."

It took less than fifteen minutes to Strangeways Jail where he was allocated a primitive cell.

Andrew sat heavily on the filthy bed and wondered how, if ever, he would leave this awful place alive. Eventually, he fell asleep, still dressed in the clothes he had been wearing when he was caught. He slept well considering the anguish caused by his predicament. He awoke at six o'clock to the sound of the cell door being unlocked. A prison officer entered followed by a figure in army uniform. At first he feigned sleep and ignored them both. That was until he recognised the voice of Major Martin Benson.

"So," Martin was saying to the prison officer, "this is the curfew violator we picked up last night."

He looked into the face of the surprised Andrew and frowned.

"We think we have caught a real trouble-maker here. He might even be guilty of treason," Martin told the prison guard. "I want him moved to an isolation cell where we can question him out of earshot of other prisoners."

"I will have to ask one of the prison governors," the man replied hesitantly.

Andrew was sure that Martin had a plan but why take him to an isolation cell?

"I have rights," Andrew interjected. "Just because I broke the curfew trying to get help for my son does not make me into a criminal."

"I am afraid it does and I believe you had no ID. You are in deep trouble Mackintosh or whatever your name is."

Martin turned to the prison guard again and said, "I will go and find a governor myself and get authority for the transfer."

The two men turned and left the cell and Andrew heard the electronic lock click back into place. He was however, relieved that Martin had witnessed his arrest. But how could his friend get him released without attracting suspicion on himself?

Ten minutes later Martin returned with the guard and said,

"Get your things, you are being transferred to an isolation cell in the high security block."

The high security block was a new building at the rear of the huge prison. It had been built in 2017 with the sole purpose of keeping 'political' prisoners away from the assorted criminals housed in the main jail. These people were treated far better than the 'politicals' and many of them were released early to serve in the police and army. The WDL government needed legions of tough, violent men to keep the general population terrorised into submission.

Although the high security block was only three years old the cells were filthy. Toilet facilities had been provided with each cell and when these failed to work no attempt was made to repair them. As a result the entire building stank and many of the prisoners became ill and died long before they could be executed. If disease did not get them, malnutrition did. This Andrew discovered after just one day of his incarceration when a breakfast and evening meal were delivered to him consisting of a glass of discoloured water and a piece of soggy toast for each meal. Lunch did not appear at all and Andrew was certain that, if it had, it would have consisted of the same menu.

However, Andrew hoped desperately that Martin would somehow find a way to save him and this thought consoled him. Had the army Captain not seen him, he knew his situation would have been completely hopeless.

A further three days went by during which Andrew's diet consisted of just water and toast and his exercise was just walking up and down the confined area of the cell, a distance of just three metres in length. He had no reading material and even his request for a pen and paper was denied. All he could do was to brood on his predicament and he knew that if Martin did not find a way to have him released quickly, his very sanity would be threatened.

On the fourth day a large contingent of prison guards went round the cells opening the doors and yelling to all the inmates to assemble outside the doorways. They were told to stand to attention with their hands clasped together in front of them. Andrew looked at the occupants of the neighbouring cells and saw that most of them were emaciated and many could hardly stand up. Then the man in the cell next door but one to him collapsed onto the concrete floor to receive a torrent of abuse from one of the guards.

Two of them tried to drag him to his feet and when this failed they threw him bodily back into his cell.

Once all the prisoners were in position, at least those capable of standing, they were marched into a large open hall where they were instructed to stand easy and await further instructions.

After half an hour or so which saw a number of other pitiful wretches collapse and be dragged away, a man who seemed to be a prison governor entered the room.

He was accompanied by three army officers and a man who appeared, from his uniform, to be a very senior policeman, possibly a Chief Constable. Then Andrew realised that one of the army officers was his friend Martin Benson. Was it just coincidence that he was there or had he somehow engineered this meeting as cover for an attempt at Andrew's escape?

Then the Governor began to speak…..

Chapter thirty

Raided

James Benson was an accountant and he worked in the offices of a large firm in the city of London. Since the WDL had become the government his work had become more and more difficult as a result of the poorly drafted torrents of new tax legislation spewed out. Much of this conflicted with older taxation law and in many cases contradicted rules issued just weeks apart from each other by the regime. However, the pay was good and he gave the senior partners, friends of the Prime Minister, the impression that he was loyal not only to the firm, but also to the government.

His routine was to leave his flat in Mayfair at seven o'clock every morning, to travel to the office via the very limited tube service that ran in the capital of WDL Britain. He would stay there all day and return on Mondays, Wednesdays and Fridays at about four o'clock in the afternoon to await the arrival of his friend Charles Charleston. On Tuesdays and Thursdays he always worked late, sometimes not returning home until eight o'clock in the evening; just an hour before the curfew.

The fateful day when the Prime Minister had discovered that his son Charles was in a homosexual relationship with James Benson, was a Tuesday and James had intended to stay late at the office as usual. However, as the morning progressed a really bad head cold took possession of him. He was unable to read the documents associated with the accounts he was working on as his eyes were streaming copiously.

In the end James decided to return home at lunch time. He had to wait nearly an hour for a train and the journey underground made a bad cold even worse. Eventually he left the train and was glad to be back on the surface and able to breathe fresher air, even if this was still in central London. He coughed and spluttered as he walked back towards his apartment and stopped in his tracks as he turned the final corner to see a jeep load of soldiers running into the block, his block, with rifles raised. His immediate thought was that his membership of the group of fifteen had been discovered. Probably someone else had been arrested, tortured and identified some or all of his co-conspirators. He stood in the doorway of a nearby store watching to see when the soldiers would leave and he could return to his home. Fortunately it was a warm day but nevertheless he longed to be back in his flat relaxing with a drop of the single malt Scotch Whisky that was a gift from his friend, the Prime Minister's son Charles. Now he had more to worry about than just a head cold. Was this raid connected to Charles or maybe to his brother Martin, the army captain?

There was a small park just around the corner and he decided eventually to go there and to try, in the privacy of the trees, to use his illegal mobile phone to call his brother.

Martin, at that time, unbeknown to James, was in Strangeways Jail in Manchester with a somewhat wild plan to secure the release of their mutual friend Andrew Robertson. His phone was thankfully switched off as, although army officers were allowed army issue mobiles, private ones, such as the one

James had tried to call him on, could have led Martin into very dangerous waters.

James knew he could not return home while the army were there. He could not contact Charles and for all he knew maybe Charles had inadvertently informed someone who would not approve, of their relationship. How right he was!

Fortunately, he always kept a thousand pounds or so in crisp £50 notes in his wallet. He would give the army another hour and if they were still 'in occupation,' he would walk round to the home of the leader of his group of fifteen. At least he had some cash on him if he needed to take alternative action such as checking into a hotel.

He arrived at the apartment block where Malcolm Grainger lived, at half past four. It was just off the Edgware Road. He was greeted by Susan, Malcolm's wife.

"Hello James," she said. "Please come in. Malcolm will be back soon and will be pleased to see you."

Just twenty five minutes later James heard brisk footsteps approaching the Grainger's lounge where he was comfortably seated. It was Malcolm who bounded into the room to welcome him.

"James, my dear fellow," he began. "So nice to see you. To what do we owe this pleasure?"

"I am afraid that I am in trouble," he explained. He then proceeded to tell Malcolm the entire story of how his brother had suggested that he cultivate the friendship of Charles Charleston. How he had formed a genuine liking for the young man and how that had led to a relationship when they discovered they were both gay and unattached.

"Either because of my association with our group of fifteen or my relationship with Charles, I was raided today by soldiers. Fortunately I saw them arrive and realising they were waiting for me, I decided not to return home and to come here."

Malcolm nodded anxiously."Are you sure you were not followed?

"Absolutely not. The soldiers never saw me and I kept well out of their sight after that. Is there some way we can contact Charles?" he enquired.

"Yes. I have his number at the Ministry of Defence," James answered. "However, I have never used it. It could be dangerous."

"I can use it," Malcolm replied. "As far as the government knows I am a loyal member of the WDL and I am an officer in the Territorial Army. I will phone Charles now and try to set up a meeting."

A minute later Charles Charleston was on the line.

"Captain Charleston," Malcolm began. "I am Major Malcolm Grainger of the Territorial Army. I would like to see you regarding a man called James Benson who wishes to join our group."

"Did you say James Benson?" Charles replied in a voice shaking with emotion.

"Yes, that's the fellah," Malcolm replied. "Do you know him?"

There was silence and heavy breathing on the other end of the line until Charles answered,

"I think we had better meet. Where are you now?"

"Edgware Road, not far from George Street," Malcolm responded.

"Can you meet me in half an hour at the café in Hyde Park near Speakers Corner?" Charles enquired anxiously.

"Captain Charleston," Malcolm replied. "Of course I can meet you but I need to know if there is a problem with James Benson as I would not like to think that I was having contact with anyone who did not have the approval of the WDL and the army."

"Major Grainger," Charles answered. "I will explain everything when I see you but be assured you were absolutely right to contact me and I commend you for your action."

"Something is wrong," Malcolm told James as they passed the many boarded-up Arab restaurants that used to thrive on this road.

"However, I don't think he is at all suspicious of me. But he certainly sounds upset. The trick will be trying to get him to open up and tell me his problem. Then maybe I can discover if it has any connection with what has happened to you."

The café was just a fifteen minute stroll from Malcolm Grainger's flat and James and Malcolm arrived before Charles Charleston.

Charles was his in army uniform which was his normal mode of dress at the Defence Ministry. However, his demeanour was decidedly un-soldier like. He was by nature gentle and caring and in fact the complete antithesis of his father. He was also of a nervous disposition and that was probably the result of a life-time of bullying by Colonel Charleston. He approached the table where Malcolm was sitting and enquired if he was indeed Major Grainger. James, at this juncture was out of sight at another table round the corner from where Malcolm was sitting.

"Ah, so you must be Captain Charleston?" Malcolm replied. "Please, do sit down. Can I get you a coffee?"

Charles shook his head. How could he drink coffee when the life of his 'special' friend James was in danger?

"Right now," Malcolm began. "You have some information about James Benson that might affect his suitability to be in the Territorials?"

"When did you last speak to him?" Charles demanded.

"This afternoon," Malcolm replied.

"This afternoon," Charles repeated, "and did he seem to be alright?"

"Yes, of course," Malcolm answered. "Why ever should he not be?"

"What time was it when you spoke to him?" Charles asked.

"Oh, just about an hour ago," Malcolm replied.

"I need to speak to him about another matter but have been unable to do so," Charles explained.

"I see," Malcolm commented gravely. "Does this mean he is in trouble?"

"No," Charles stammered. "At least, not with me."

This chap Grainger seems a decent sort, he decided.

"Look I need to see him urgently on a personal matter. If you know where he is, can you put me in touch with him?"

Malcolm surveyed his younger companion. He seemed to be totally sincere.

"Look if I put you in touch do I have your word that no harm will come to him?"

"Absolutely," Charles replied. "You have my word as an army officer."

Malcolm nearly burst out laughing when he heard this statement. He remembered when being an army officer implied you were a man of your word. Sadly this description did not apply to ninety nine per cent of the officers in the British army in WDL Britain.

"Just a moment," Malcolm said, rising from the chair. "I will be back in a moment."

Charles looked terrified. *Was this Malcolm working for his father? Had he fallen into a trap set by the Prime Minister to catch him trying to be in contact with James?*

Charles suddenly felt a gentle tap on the shoulder and looked round to see James Benson.

"Is that seat taken?" James enquired.

"Oh, thank God you are alright," was all Charles could say.

In the meantime Malcolm had paid for his coffee and approached the table to bid farewell to the close friends.

"If you ever need my help again, either of you, do not hesitate to get in touch," he told them.

They were now the only customers in the café and as soon as Malcolm was out of earshot, Charles and James exchanged stories. First Charles told James of how his father had arranged to have him watched and thus discovered their relationship. He told James that his father had instructed him never again to see him. Then James told Charles of the arrival of the military and of the incredible piece of luck that prevented him from returning later in the day when the tell-tale army vehicle would have been long since gone. He would then have entered the flat to find soldiers waiting to arrest him and that, without doubt would have been the end of him.

"It is a terrible thing to say," Charles told his friend, "but I really hate my father. I am neither blind nor stupid and I have seen, for some years now, how he treats the people of this country. He is a power-mad bully and the sooner he is removed as a tyrant, the happier I will be."

"We must leave London at once," James replied without commenting on what his friend had just said. "Have you any money? I have enough to pay for travel and I would like to take you to my brother who is now in Manchester."

They both knew that inter-city travel was no longer a simple matter. There were occasional trains and long distance coaches but travellers needed a permit to leave their own area. The two men were aware that, without a shadow of a doubt, police and troops at the stations would be on the lookout for James Benson and probably also for Charles Charleston. The latter had no idea of how to cope with these problems. He had always been able to travel without restriction as the Prime Minister's son and an officer in the British army. Fortunately James had lived before on the edge of the law as a member of a group of fifteen.

"You do realise that I am now a wanted man and so will you be, before long," he told Charles. "We cannot just go and jump on a train. However what we have to do is to go to a lorry park and look for any truck owned by Fred Harrison. We then ask which is his Manchester overnight truck and they will take us. The charge will be about £200 each and I can cover that if you do not have the money."

"Ok," Charles said, "But I do have some money, so there is no problem there. Manchester here we come."

Chapter thirty one

Interviewing

"We are to be greatly honoured later this morning to be receiving a visit from Colonel Sidney Charleston, the Prime Minister," the Governor announced. "Together with Captain Martin Benson he will personally interview five men. The Captain will read out the names after I have finished and the rest of you can then return to your cells,"

"I want no noise he told the half-dead wretches. Anyone who makes a disturbance while the Colonel is here can expect severe punishment."

So what was the treatment they had endured up till now? Andrew thought.

Then Captain Martin Benson stepped forward. "These are the five men who are to remain here after the others return to their cells. Owen Williams, Patrick O'Reilly, Jonathan Mackintosh (the name Andrew had been arrested under,) George Chapman and Phillip Broadhurst. Step forward you five!"

Andrew surveyed his companions. They were all recent arrivals and still in reasonable health.

All the other prisoners now walked, staggered or were dragged back to the cells.

Then Martin Benson spoke again.

"The Prime Minister has decided to give an early release to just one of you men. Which one, I have no idea. He will interview you individually and then decide your suitability to work under his direct control in London. His decision will be based on which of you can most readily be rehabilitated as a useful member of society. Political prisoners do not usually get this opportunity but the Colonel is a generous man and it is quite amazing that he has personally taken time away from the affairs of state to give this wonderful chance to one of you."

The Chief Constable, the Governor and the other two army officers now set off for the entrance to the jail to await the arrival of the 'distinguished' visitor.

This left the five men with Captain Benson and some twenty prison officers guarding the entrances to the hall.

"Right, men," Martin Benson told them. "This will be the drill. First the Prime Minister will enter with the other distinguished visitors. You will all stand to attention. Then he will make a short speech and finally he will be escorted by me to that office over there." Captain Benson pointed in the direction of a doorway.

"Then I will return and call out your names, one at a time and escort each of you into the office for a private interview. Is that all understood?"

"Yes Sir," the five bewildered men said in unison.

Ten minutes later a prison officer entered the hall and approached Captain Benson.

"Yes!" the army captain exclaimed in a rough voice. "What is it?"

"Sir," the guard replied, "the Prime Minister has arrived. He is being taken to the governor's office for a drink and snack before coming over to the hall."

Oh, my goodness, Martin thought. *I just hope Jeremy can cope. Socialising with the governor was never in the plan. He has had so little time to practice the role and he could so easily blow it and what if they offer him food that is not Kosher?*

But he need not have worried. The 'Prime Minister' was clean shaven (of course) and wearing his usual uniform as colonel of the regiment. He strode along with the governor with his characteristic swagger. He had spent the previous three days listening to recordings of Charleston's voice and watching videos of the way he moved.

Once inside the governor's office he seated himself in a chair and looked ostentatiously at his watch.

"Well Mr Governor," he said. "We have five minutes and then I want to get on with these cursed interviews. You know, I do not know what possessed me to get involved in this stunt but maybe the prisoner I choose will be useful to me. He had better be or everyone will be for the high jump and that includes you."

The governor looked at him uncomfortably and offered him a drink.

"Would you like a drop of single malt sir?" he enquired soothingly.

"Well just a small one and then let's get on with this nonsense," the 'PM' replied, giving the governor a glare.

The two army officers were waiting outside the governor's office when the pair came out.

"I don't know what you are hanging about for," the 'PM' muttered.

"Go and do something useful. The governor knows his way around the place without you two and we are in a high security prison. I don't need protecting in here. In any case there are plenty of prison officers around if there is any trouble."

"Well come on, man" he continued, addressing the governor again. "Let's get on with it."

As soon as they entered the hall Captain Benson marched smartly up to them and saluted.

"An honour to have you here sir," he said. "Please follow me into an office that has been prepared for the interviews."

The 'Prime Minister' turned again to the governor and airily dismissed him.

"Well come on then!" he addressed Martin impatiently. "Let's make a start. I am sure this will be a colossal waste of time but once I am settled you can send in the first candidate."

The first candidate was Owen Williams. He was a Welsh nationalist who deeply resented the English domination of his country. He would probably have been in trouble with a democratic Westminster regime and his pronouncements before he was apprehended made it certain that under the tyrannical rule of the WDL, his days were numbered. The 'PM' was furious and made a point of severely criticising Martin Benson for wasting his time. This was of course said in the earshot of the governor, hovering by the newly opened office door.

Then came Patrick O'Reilly who turned out not even to be a British subject. He was a national of the Irish Republic and although also a trouble-maker he certainly did not deserve the fate that almost inevitably awaited him.

The next man was Andrew Robertson who, like the first two, was marched into the office by Captain Benson and then the door was firmly closed.

"You told me you could never do this," Andrew said in a low voice. "In truth you are brilliant."

Jeremy allowed himself the first and only smile of that harrowing day and then proceeded to interrogate Andrew in the same loud voice he had used for the first two candidates. Having dismissed the Welshman and the Irishman in five minutes each he spend twenty minutes with Andrew and then told him to wait outside with the others.

The final two were also given longer interviews. Jeremy was genuinely interested in how solid respectable Englishmen had finished up in this hell-hole. He would have been delighted to have taken all five away with him but there was only one purpose for this whole charade, to secure the freedom of Andrew Robertson (Jonathan Mackintosh.)

The five men were now back together again and waiting anxiously for the verdict. Owen Williams and Patrick O'Reilly were both very downcast as they were certain after their interviews that they had no chance of being chosen. The remaining three men, all English could only hope that their answers would have impressed the Prime Minister sufficiently to choose one of them. Of course one of them knew for certain that he would be the one to be released but the dread at what the verdict would be, for the others, must have been infectious and he felt the same numbing terror as they did.

Then the wait was over. The 'Prime Minister' turned to Martin.

"Captain Benson, never, ever again involve me in a scheme like this. I have much better things to do with my time. As for the first two candidates, I would like to know who chose them as they are totally unsuitable. The other three are obviously men of education and intelligence. In the interviews they indicated they could and would work with the WDL for a better Britain. However, the plan is to release only one at this stage and that must be Jonathan Mackintosh. Step forward man," he continued.

For a moment Andrew failed to realise who they were talking about until he reminded himself that this was the name he had given himself when arrested for breaking the curfew. Naturally that was how he was known in jail.

"Mackintosh, you will leave this prison with Captain Benson who will arrange your transport to London. There you will receive further instructions. And never again try to break the curfew. Do you understand that even in matters of life and death you are forbidden to leave your home at night."

Jeremy was tempted to say that he hoped that the sick child, the excuse for curfew breaking, would recover and then he reminded himself that Sidney Charleston would never have shown even that much humanity.

The 'Prime Minister' turned on his heel and, accompanied by the governor, he swaggered out of the hall to hurriedly depart from the prison in a waiting limousine.

The governor then returned to his own office and this was where Captain Benson now marched with his new charge. Release papers were signed in the name of Jonathan Mackintosh and half an hour later Martin and Andrew walked out of the gates to a waiting car.

As the vehicle sped away the governor received a phone call from the Mayor of Manchester, Thomas Appleby. They were good friends and the governor was always pleased to hear from his pal.

"Hello Thomas," he began. "Good to hear from you. What can I do for you?"

"Did you say that the Prime Minister himself was visiting your establishment today?" the mayor enquired in a puzzled voice.

"Yes, he came earlier this morning and has now departed in his limousine. I assume he will be calling on you," the governor replied.

"He will have a job! I just saw him in a live TV broadcast from London."

"But that is impossible, he was here. I talked to him. I gave him a glass of my best single malt. You must be mistaken. He left after arranging the release of a prisoner. I think you need to check your facts. It must have been a recorded programme you saw," the governor suggested.

"I will phone through to Downing Street now," Mayor Appleby replied.

A few moments later the phone rang again on the governor's desk.

"Well I don't know who you had there but it certainly wasn't the PM," Thomas Appleby told him.

"That cannot be. It was definitely him. He looked like the colonel; he sounded like the colonel and he acted like the colonel."

"Well I just spoke to him myself," the mayor replied. "You have been taken for a ride. Did you say he arranged for a prisoner to be released? If so, who was he?"

The governor was becoming increasingly frightened as the conversation progressed. If he had been dealing with an imposter, how could he have looked so much like Charleston?

"I hope you did not mention any of this to the Colonel," the governor replied. "And I have just remembered he was with an army officer Major Martin Benson."

"You have still not told me the name of the man who was released," the mayor commented.

"His name was Jonathan Mackintosh," the governor answered in a low voice. "Please tell me that you did not mention anything about me and the prison to the PM."

"As it happens I thought something was wrong so I decided I had better speak to you again first. I have never heard of Jonathan Mackintosh but I do know Captain Benson. He is an old army pal of the PM. A loyal WDL man, as far as I know. Listen you have definitely been had but it is nothing to do with me. You had better contact Captain Benson. It all looks very murky to me but maybe he can throw some light on what has been going on under your nose."

An investigation took place. The governor was accused of gross incompetence and now resides in his own jail. Andrew Robertson lived to fight another day and Rabbi Jeremy Pearson returned to his flock.

Sadly, Captain Martin Benson disappeared (at least from the army.) He joined his friend Andrew in the underworld where they both strived to free Britain from the curse of the colonel and his infernal political machine the WDL. But how could this be achieved?

CHAPTER THIRTY TWO

A TRUCK TRIP

James Benson and Charles Charleston were shocked when they arrived at the Lorry Park, as the area was crawling with soldiers.

They soon spotted one of Fred Harrison's trucks but could not risk approaching it. Obviously the police and the army knew just as well as they did that this was the only way to travel between cities without a permit. As a result they constantly raided lorry parks looking for dissidents. There was a disused wooden shed at the end of the park and the two men made their way over to it, managing to keep out of sight by dodging between the huge high-sided vehicles.

The door of the shed was locked. They could not risk any noise that they might make trying to force it open and thus be heard and picked up by the patrols, so they crouched down and waited. It was ten o'clock, one hour after curfew when the last police cars and jeeps left and by this time many of the trucks had trundled off to start their journeys.

They decided to try again and find one of the trucks of the Fred Harrison fleet and they carefully made their way between the rows of the remaining lorries. The lorry they had seen earlier had now departed and they hoped against hope that was not the Manchester truck. A further half hour passed and then they saw parked on its own, away to the left, the truck they sought. When they arrived alongside the cab of the vehicle the curtains were closed and James gently reached up to knock on the driver's door. At first that met with no response and then the curtain opened. A figure with about a week's growth of beard surveyed them and then opened the window.

"What do you two want?" he demanded.

"We were told to ask for the Manchester overnight truck," Charles explained.

"And what would you want with it?" the driver asked.

"Look, is it here or has it gone?" James said.

"And what would you want with it?" the driver again asked suspiciously.

"We are looking for a lift," Charles explained.

"Surely army officers don't need to take lifts like this," he commented. "You have all the vehicles you need and the drivers to take you wherever you want to go."

It was only then that Charles realised that he was still in uniform. James, also looked a highly unlikely type to be trying to hitch a lift in a truck. He was still in his city suit.

Suddenly the driver flung open the door of the cab and jumped to the ground.

"I don't know what you two guys are about but I can tell you I am not going to fall for it," he told them. "I am going to get a cup of coffee and then I am off. I suggest you go back to your bosses and tell them that Fred Harrison Trucks doesn't give illegal lifts. Have you got that?"

Having finished his little speech he locked the truck and marched off angrily.

James and Charles looked at one another.

"Now what do we do?"

"All we can do is wait for this guy to return and try to explain that we are on the run," James said.

"However, if he turns out to be a WDL man, we will be in big trouble but I don't see what else we can do."

Just ten minute went by when the two men heard the sound of footsteps hurrying towards them. They quickly made their way round to the rear of truck to hide from view and to see who was approaching and were surprised to see that it was the driver.

"If you are still here and hiding, you can come out. I have just heard all about you on the radio and I can help," he called in a hoarse whisper that just carried far enough for them to hear,

Charles and James peered at the man and decided that they would have to take their chances with him. They walked warily back towards him.

As they approached he grinned and nodded.

"It is ok, if those bastards from the army are after you I will give you a lift. I am going to Manchester. My name is Jack Johnson. At least you picked the right truck!" he told them. "You will have to get in the back and make yourself as comfortable as possible between the cartons. However, I can give you some cans of coke and some biscuits," he continued.

Neither man was accustomed to anything but home comforts but they knew that the back of the truck, sitting on the hard wooden floor between huge cartons, was infinitely preferable to being flung into a filthy jail cell.

Six hours later they arrived in Manchester and faced an even bigger quandary.

CHAPTER THIRTY THREE

AN UNLIKELY SAVIOUR

The PM was furious. His younger son had disappeared from the radar and so had Charles' boy friend James Benson. How his own flesh and blood could have turned out to be a pervert, astonished him. He considered himself a tolerant man. Didn't he accept people of all races as long as they towed the party line? Gays, however, were completely beyond the pale. *He is no longer my son,* he decided. *When the police or army catch him, they can throw them both into prison and they can rot there together for all I care.*

Apart from the problem of his son Charles, there was another matter aggravating him. Someone had had the impertinence to impersonate him in a visit to a Manchester prison. And even worse, they had managed to facilitate the escape of a prisoner. Then there was his deep disappointment with Captain Martin Benson. He had been part of this plot to release the dangerous criminal. He remembered Martin well. He had been an excellent soldier and had served his country well. Now, for some inexplicable reason he had turned against his own Colonel. He had to be found and punished as an example of what happened to traitors.

After brooding on these matters he decided he needed cheering up. He would go and see his grandson and then, once the child was in bed he would spend some very satisfying quality time with Tricia, his daughter-in-law. She knew just how to relieve the tensions that arose from being head of state.

It was after midnight when he left Tricia and his grandson's quarters and returned to his own private flat within the Downing Street complex. Justine was sitting in the lounge staring into space.

"You certainly spend a lot of time with your grandson," she said, seething. "I thought children were usually tucked up in bed by seven or eight o'clock."

Predictably the colonel lost his cool.

"How dare you question me after what you did at that party," he shouted. "I have had quite enough of you. You can get out now."

He marched into the bedroom and started to throw her clothes on to the bed.

Justine may have known the PM for many years but whatever knack she may have had in soothing his tempers had long since disappeared. A few minutes later she was out on the street with just a few of her essential belongings packed in a small suitcase.

Downing Street was cordoned off from the rest of London by high fences and even higher gates. Government personnel and their families within the area could move around the compound as they wished and were not subject to the curfew.

It was a warm evening and she stood in the street pondering what to do. She was homeless and in addition she had now lost access to her ultimate target. When the signal came to overthrow this tyrannical government she would be unable to play her part. Her associates in the group of fifteen would be deeply disappointed.

Where could she go at this time of night? She dare not leave Downing Street as she would then inevitably be picked up by the police for breaking the curfew. Then help arrived from a totally unexpected source.

Justine heard the sound of high heeled shoes clicking along the street and suddenly she recognised the owner as her predecessor in the heart (if he had one) and the bed of her husband, Daphne Charleston; the divorced ex-wife of the Prime Minister.

Daphne stared at Justine in amazement.

"Hello," she said. "What on earth are you doing out here?"

Justine considered herself to be fairly tough but with the predicament she was now in, she burst in to tears.

Daphne had long since realised that she had the best of both worlds. She never had to endure any contact with her ex-husband who she now totally despised. However, at the request of her two sons she had been allocated a small apartment in Downing Street and lived there comfortably enough. The problem now was that Edgar had been posted to the north of England and she had just heard that there had been trouble between Charles and his father which had resulted in him leaving his home within the compound. What that trouble was, she did not know but she was determined to find out. As for Justine, she pitied anyone forced to live with Sidney. Furthermore, she was convinced that the PM was having a relationship with Tricia, their 'tart of a daughter-in-law,' as she regarded her.

She put her arms around Justine and tried to comfort her.

"Sidney has thrown me out," she sobbed.

"Well you can stay with me to night," Daphne replied. "Come on, we can talk inside."

Once inside Daphne's apartment, her hostess poured a large cognac for her house-guest and seated in elegant armchairs opposite each other the pair began to talk.

"What on earth happened? It must have been bad if he threw you out. I thought you two were really solid," Daphne commented.

"I had the impertinence to accuse him of having an affair," Justine explained.

"Can I talk to you frankly?" Daphne began.

Justine nodded, still feeling tearful.

"When I married Sidney I knew he was tough and determined. I also thought that if he was ever elected to the position he now holds, he would be a tremendous power for good for the people. How wrong I was," she continued. "The only person he has been good for, is himself, Sidney Charleston. And of course his evil cronies."

Justine began to feel better. She wondered whether she could risk telling Daphne about the group of fifteen.

"Do you know there is a huge undercurrent of hatred in the country for Sidney and what he has done to Britain?" she asked Daphne. "There are active groups secretly planning how they can rid the country of Sidney and the WDL."

"I knew there must be," Daphne replied. "I would love to be part of that. He may be the father of my children but I could never forget what he did to my father. He died in prison, you know."

Justine nodded.

"Anyway, you must be exhausted after the traumatic evening you have had. I will show you your room and we can talk some more in the morning."

It took Justine a long time to fall asleep. She was away from the husband she detested and she now had a new friend. The fact that her new friend was the woman she supplanted as the wife of Sidney Charleston struck her as incredibly bizarre. But Daphne was her saviour. What on earth would she have done if she had not appeared?

The two women breakfasted together and Justine told Daphne about her group of fifteen. She had been enrolled by Malcolm Grainger who had also enrolled James Benson. She did not, of course mention any names and indeed apart from Malcolm she did not know the identity of any of her fellow members.

Justine had her own group and in fact there was a vacancy due to one member managing to escape from Britain with a suitcase of cash.

She asked Daphne if we would like to join.

"At the moment," she explained, "we are just recruiting. Anyone who wants to see the back of this government can join as long as we are convinced of his or her sincerity. When the time comes to act, you will be told what is required."

"Please count me in," Daphne replied. "I will gladly do whatever is needed. And when my older son Edgar hears what is going on with his wife, he will also be a candidate. As for Charles, I would love to recruit him but I do not know where he is. It is two days now since anyone has seen him and I am becoming very concerned."

After breakfast Daphne turned on the closed circuit television that served the party faithful and waited for the news. They did not have long to wait.

"Here is a special announcement from the Prime Minister, Colonel Sidney Charleston," the news reader stated in his sanctimonious tone.

"A plot to assassinate our leader Colonel Charleston has been discovered. The two main organisers of this plot are James Benson, a known homosexual living in Mayfair and Charles Charleston, the Prime Minister's younger son. As will be readily understood the fact that a member of his own family could be involved in such traitorous activities is deeply distressing. If you see these men do not approach them as they are dangerous. Please report their presence directly to a member of the police or the armed forces."

The two women surveyed each other in a mixture of shock and horror.

Daphne spoke first. "Did you notice the use of the term 'a known homosexual'? I am sure you know how Sidney hates gays," she said. "I have wondered myself for some time if that was Charles sexual preference. Whenever I have seen him and asked him about girl friends, he has always ended the conversation abruptly. I am sure," she continued, "that is the problem. Charles would never hurt a fly, let alone his own father. Sidney has discovered that Charles is gay and, son or not, he is now determined to get rid of him. I rather suspect that this James Benson must be his boy friend."

"Of course I know Charles well enough. We all live here and Charles did come to visit his father fairly frequently, at least until recently," Justine added. "That will have been when he started this affair with, what was his name, James Benson? That man, your ex and my husband, is evil incarnate and how we both could have originally thought we loved him, is impossible to understand."

"Well, this is the final straw," Daphne said. "He has to be stopped one way or another. I am worried sick now about Charles. Where can he be? There must be something I can do to protect him. There are no words to describe the hatred that Sidney is now showing against my son." She began to cry and Justine crossed over to Daphne to try and comfort her.

Sidney was stoking up the fires of hatred against him, even among those who had been closest to him. The two women knew he had to be stopped, but how?

Chapter thirty four

Jenkins Avenue

Jack Johnson, the truck driver was as good as his word. At five thirty the following morning he pulled on to a lorry park in the borough of Bury in the north of Greater Manchester. He went round to the rear of the large vehicle and found his two passengers hidden behind a stack of huge cartons.

"Well, we are here," he said. "Whereabouts in Manchester are you heading for?"

"We have to find my brother," James explained. "He has recently been posted here from the north. I have an address in Prestwich."

"Well take it easy guys," Jack answered. "I am afraid that if you are on the run, you need to travel at busy times when the streets are crowded. Look," he continued, "I can take you down towards Prestwich if that will help as I have one delivery down there and then I will make for the motorway again after breakfast."

"We really cannot thank you enough," James said. He took out his wallet. "How much do I owe you?" he enquired.

"Nothing," Jack replied. "I am glad to be able to help. I do not care what the government and the police are saying about you. I can see for myself that you are decent guys. That is what is happening in this country; decent people are being made into criminals."

"I really must insist on paying you," James replied. "You have literally saved our lives."

"I said no payment and I meant no payment!" the truck driver answered. "You will need all your money while you are on the run."

"I am going to stop in the car park of a large supermarket where I have to make a delivery. When I open the doors again you can get out. But just be careful that no one sees you or we will all be in deep trouble."

Half an hour later James and Charles were mingling with crowds of shoppers in the store. They were desperately thirsty and rather hungry. There was a short queue for tables at the coffee shop adjoining and they eventually managed to order a substantial breakfast. After that the world looked a somewhat better place although they knew that they were still in constant danger.

They bought a map of the area and easily located Jenkins Avenue where James' brother Martin had told him, only ten days earlier, that he would be living. It looked like no more than half an hour's walk and they set off. They walked fairly slowly and chatted inconsequentially as they strode along. This was so that any police or army patrols that passed them by would not see anything strange in their behaviour. The security forces were always suspicious of people who appeared to be in a hurry.

Eventually they arrived and made their way towards number 27. James knew his brother Martin was a Captain in the army but it had occurred to him that the police could still be waiting for him there, knowing the relationship. However, they had nowhere else to go in Manchester that offered any kind of safe haven.

After watching the house for a few minutes it was decided that Charles should approach on his own. If the police were there they would be looking for two men and one the brother of Martin. He rang the bell three times but it was obvious no one was in. Charles thought this a little strange as James had told him that Martin had a wife and two young children. However, he decided they could be out shopping. He felt that it would be dangerous to draw unnecessary attention to himself by banging noisily on the door. This could alert the neighbours and lead to problems. In any case he could hear the bell ringing inside the house each time he pressed the push button, surely, if anyone was in, they would have heard it.

He decided to leave and was closing the gate to the garden path behind him when a quiet voice said,

"Can I help you?"

He looked up to see a man who had just come out of the house next door. He was wearing a large wide-brimmed black hat, a dark double-breasted suit and he sported a full beard. Two thoughts struck Charles almost simultaneously. *He must be a Rabbi* and *he looks terribly familiar to me.*

"Can I help you?" the man repeated.

Charles decided to take the plunge.

"I was looking for Captain Martin Benson," he volunteered.

"And who are you?" the man enquired. In WDL Britain people were always careful with strangers. There were far too many men and women who would sell information to the security forces in exchange for favours for them and their families.

The next thing the man said really surprised Charles.

"Would you like to come in to my house next door, to wait for him?" This sort of kindness was a rarity in a country where people were terrified to trust anyone they did not know well.

It was no accident that Rabbi Jeremy Pearson lived next door to Captain Martin Benson. They had both discussed this possibility with Andrew when the Captain and his family had been posted to Manchester. The house next door had been empty for a few months after the previous occupants had suddenly disappeared. This was not an unusual occurrence in the country under the tyrannical rule of Sidney Charleston.

Now, after the successful escape of Andrew from prison thanks to the intervention of Martin and Jeremy, Andrew and Martin were both wanted men. Martin's family was quickly despatched to relatives in the Midlands The basement under the Rabbi's house had, at some time in the past, been converted into a flat and Jeremy insisted that the two wanted men should stay there; at least until other arrangements could be made.

James watched his friend's meeting with Jeremy from a vantage point further up the road. *What on earth was James doing, going in to the house next door with a guy who looked like a Rabbi?* He pondered. All he could do was to anxiously watch and wait.

Jeremy had been desperately lonely since the killing of his wife by trigger-happy soldiers. His children were so far away and growing up hardly knowing him. However, all this sad situation did was to re-double his resolve to do what he could to help in the wrenching Britain back from the stranglehold of Sidney Charleston and his associates. That was why, when his help was needed he had agreed at once to help to rescue Andrew from prison.

At least now, he was no longer alone in the house. Once it was dark and the curtains were drawn Andrew and Martin came up from the basement each evening. They had much to discuss.

On the night before Charles suddenly arrived next door, the three men were sitting round the Rabbi's table making plans for the final showdown with Charleston. Only Martin had a mobile and that was an illegal one. His military one had finished up in the river Irwell soon after leaving the jail with Jeremy. However, it was against the law to possess a mobile phone in WDL Britain unless you were a member of the government, local government, senior member of the WDL, police or military. Unauthorised phones were easily traced and located if switched on and as a result, Martin only activated his every few hours and then only for a few minutes at a time to check for messages. At nine thirty that evening he had switched on to find a text message from Malcolm Grainger in London. It was to alert him to the fact that Martin's brother James Benson and Charles Charleston were on the run and could quite conceivably be on their way to Manchester and if so would obviously contact them.

"Charles Charleston!" Andrew commented, "that sounds like one of the dear Colonel's sons. What has he been up to that has offended daddy?"

Charles followed Jeremy into his house and was rather shocked when, as soon as the front door was closed, he heard the Rabbi demand,

"Where is your friend James?"

Charles went white and Jeremy realised that the unexpected question must have frightened him.

"Sorry, I meant to say I do know who you are and it was a gentleman called Malcolm Grainger who alerted us to expect you both. Don't worry, you are among friends here."

Charles nodded a little uncertainly.

"My name is Rabbi Jeremy Pearson and this evening you will be able to meet James' brother Martin who is now, like you, on the run. You will also meet another gentleman whose identity will be explained in due course."

Charles decided that he had to take a chance on this man. He said he was a Rabbi and he did not see anyone from the police or army dressing up that way to catch them. When all was said and done, neither of them was Jewish.

"James is waiting just down the road. I will go and tell him to come over," he volunteered.

He left the house and crossed the road to the corner where he knew James was hiding.

"What on earth is going on?" James demanded.

Charles told his friend of the conversation he had just had with the Rabbi.

"How do you know he is really who he says he is and that his story is true?" James demanded.

"Well, for one thing, if he was from the security services he would not have let me go," Charles suggested. "I reckon this guy is on the level."

"We can't stay here forever. I just hope you are right to trust him. Come on then, introduce me to your new friend," James replied.

CHAPTER THIRTY FIVE

EXCHANGING INFORMATION

Sidney had personally escorted his wife Justine to the door of number 10 Downing Street and dumped her suitcase on the pavement outside. He had no idea where she would go from there and he certainly did not care what happened to her. He was sure she would leave the government compound and then he would receive a phone call telling him she had been picked up by the police as a curfew breaker. He had really looked forward to that and to having the pleasure of telling the officer that she was no longer his wife and if she broke the law she must be dealt with like any other criminal. Thanks to Daphne, he was very disappointed.

During her first day as a house-guest Justine discussed with Daphne where she should now go.

"I must leave here tomorrow," she said. "If Sidney finds you are sheltering me, we will both be thrown out and I do not want the responsibility of causing you such a serious problem."

"Obviously, if he discovered that you were here, I would be in trouble but how is he to find out if we keep a low profile until we arrange something else? He never visits this apartment. If fact he has never, ever been here," Daphne replied. "Anyway, where would you go? Do you have any ideas?"

"I have been turning this over in mind. My only relatives are in Wales and I have had no contact with them since my mother died ten years ago," Justine explained. "I have one or two ex-boyfriends here in London and one girl friend. Sidney made sure I never saw them and I do not know what kind of a reception I would get if I contacted them now."

"Look, there is no pressure for a few days, as long as you don't mind staying inside," Daphne answered. "After being married to Sidney a rest would probably do you the world of good anyway. At least in here we also have television even if all the news is doctored. So that is settled. You are staying here for a few more days."

Colonel Sidney Charleston was mystified. Justine had just disappeared off the face of the earth. *Maybe someone was sheltering her here, inside the compound?* But who would do that? She was not the most popular person, or at least that was the way he saw her. It did not occur to him that any normal friends she might have had would be repelled by the idea of being in HIS company. She could not have left the compound, so where was she? He considered all the people he knew that she ever had any kind of contact with inside the compound and rejected them all. None of them would dare to give shelter to someone who was now his enemy. He then thought about the family. Edgar was in the north and Charles on the run, in any case they would never have given sanctuary to the woman who had replaced their mother as the PMs wife. Finally he thought about his ex-wife Daphne but he dismissed that idea as totally preposterous.

Eventually he decided that she must have managed to avoid capture as a curfew breaker after leaving that night and was now probably being sheltered by some dissident.

Daphne still had a car. An ancient relic from the days when her sons were schoolboys. It had been purchased in 2004 and she still used it for occasional shopping trips. All the security personnel knew the vehicle well and used to snigger when they recognised it and its occupant.

"There goes the PM's ex in her old banger," they would say, nudging one another.

After four days Justine and Daphne had a plan. Daphne would drive Justine out of the compound at ten thirty the following morning. Justine would crouch down on the floor behind the front seats to be out of sight. Daphne would then take her to Malcolm Grainger. He would be only too pleased to help; particularly when he realised who she was.

The plan succeeded and half an hour after leaving Downing Street, Daphne braked the car to a halt in a small entry way just off George Street. Justine was stiff from lying on the floor of the car but the short walk to Malcolm's apartment disposed of her aches and pains. In any case she was far more terrified by the possibility of being recognised than she was worried by a little discomfort.

Malcolm opened the door of his apartment and the two women were somewhat shocked to see him in the uniform of an officer in the Territorial Army.

"Hello Daphne," he began after ushering them inside and quickly and quietly closing the door.

"What brings you here?" He looked at Justine somewhat suspiciously.

"You know too many visitors draws attention to me and my family" he continued, "and there is one

WDL spy and possibility more on this floor of the building."

"Why are you wearing that uniform?" she countered. "I had an awful shock when I saw you dressed like that."

"That is my cover," Malcolm quickly assured her. "Now why are you here? Much as I am pleased to see you, you know quite well that it is only in an emergency that we contact each other directly."

"This is an emergency," Daphne replied. "Do you know who this is?"

Malcolm began to feel that he had been less than courteous.

"Please introduce me," he replied.

"This is Justine Charleston, current wife of our dear Prime Minister."

A look of horror swept over Malcolm's face.

"So you are the present Mrs Charleston?" he demanded, looking straight at Justine.

"I was, or I suppose legally I still am," she ventured. "However, my husband threw me out a few days ago when I accused him of having an affair with his daughter-in-law."

"I found her out on the street, Downing Street to be exact. I know only too well what life with dear Sidney is like and I invited her to stay with me for a few days," Daphne continued the narrative.

"Look, ladies," Malcolm said visibly shedding his troubled expression. "Come in the lounge and have a drink and let us discuss this rather interesting conundrum you have presented me with."

If this situation is used sensibly it could be to great advantage, he decided.

Once settled in Malcolm's comfortable lounge and sipping cups of hot coffee, the discussion began.

"Tell me Justine," their host asked. "May I call you Justine?"

"Yes of course," she replied.

"Please tell me why your husband suddenly decided to sever your relationship."

"I am absolutely certain that he has been having an affair with Tricia, the wife of his older son Edgar," she explained. "He sent Edgar away to the north-east a few months ago on a pretext that he was needed to deal with trouble there. Once he was out of the way Sidney visited Edgar and Tricia's quarters every evening. He says it is to see his grandson but he never returns until after midnight."

"Yes that does sound rather suspicious, to put it mildly," Malcolm commented. "Do you have any other evidence?"

"Well yes, but it is rather personal and embarrassing. Although he has demanded sex with me from time to time his enthusiasm has tended to rather flag since these visits to Tricia became a regular part of his timetable."

"Tell me," Malcolm questioned, "how do you feel about Sidney. I think it fairly unlikely, but if he suddenly wanted you back, how would you feel about it."

"I detest the man," Justine told him. "I am a Cambridge graduate but he has for some time now, treated me like a whore. He left me at a dinner a few months ago and, having had a few drinks, I did rather make a spectacle of myself with a man who danced with me most of the evening. However, it was so refreshing to be treated like a human being not just a sex object that I am afraid I behaved rather badly. Sidney was, of course told and after that, the way he treated me went from bad to worse."

"And how do you feel about the way he runs the country?" Malcolm asked.

"I have been disgusted and horrified by the way he has progressively abused his power," she explained. "I was his secretary when this whole idea of a new party, the WDL, was mooted and then activated. I thought we were all going to do wonderful things for the country. Instead he has ruined Britain and the lives of our people."

"This is nothing new," Malcolm replied. "Why did you not leave him sooner?"

"I really wanted to do so but then I was approached by some people, they would never identify themselves, and they asked me to stay with Sidney until the time came to overthrow his evil regime. How I have managed to stay there and be his wife for all this time, I really do not know. Every day, I wanted to run, but to where?"

Justine began to weep and Daphne crossed the room to try and comfort her.

"Now there is something I must tell you," Malcolm confided.

He proceeded to recount the story of Charles Charleston and his homosexual friend. Finally he explained that he had just heard from his contact in Manchester that they were now with this man and his associates.

"I am deliberately not telling you any of the names of my friends. If you would be prepared to work with us in overthrowing Sidney and his evil gang, you will eventually get to know some of them. However, we only divulge names on a need to know basis."

"Anything, anything I can do, I will gladly undertake," Justine answered still somewhat tearfully.

"Well, the first thing we have to do is to get you in touch with Edgar Charleston. This will not be easy to organise but you will need to see him face-to-face and tell him about what is going on with his father and his wife."

Justine nodded and secretly began to worry about undertaking such a delicate task. Maybe Edgar would not believe her. There had never been much love lost between either of the Colonel's sons and the woman who was responsible for their father divorcing their mother. *Maybe he won't believe me,* she pondered, *but I want Daphne and Malcolm to know that I am on their side, so I must agree to the task.*

As events transpired this was one task not required of her but other, even more difficult ones were ahead.

"My wife Susan will be in soon and we can all have a bite of lunch together," Malcolm continued. "then I will tell you my plan."

CHAPTER THIRTY SIX

A SUMMONS

The Rabbi opened the front door of the house and ushered them quickly inside.

"Follow me," he instructed and escorted them into his study.

There were two men seated there and one of the men jumped up instantly and embraced James.

"How are you my dear brother?" he enquired.

"Well enough, considering," James replied, "and how is my big brother Martin?"

"Then you must be Charles Charleston," the other man said.

"Yes, that's me," the Prime Minister's younger son replied with a rueful grin. "Not that my surname is anything to be proud of!"

"Gentlemen," the Rabbi said, "my name is Rabbi Jeremy Pearson, and my other two friends are Martin Benson and Andrew Robertson."

"I think we should have a bite of lunch and then get down to business," Jeremy continued.

The two visitors nodded gratefully.

Then the Rabbi said something very strange.

"This is itching so much, do you mind if I take it off?" And with that he literally unpeeled the full black beard that had covered most of his face.

The two original occupants of the room simply grinned while Charles and James surveyed the now clean-shaven Rabbi in horror.

"Father!" Charles stuttered peering into the Rabbi's face. "It is you isn't it?"

Jeremy began to roar with laughter.

"Well if his own son can't tell the difference that is a great comfort," Andrew said, with a grim smile.

"Don't worry Charles, I am still Rabbi Jeremy Pearson but I do look rather like your father, don't I?"

"Look like him!" Charles gasped, "I can't believe you are not him. There are just two things that persuade me to believe you all. My father never laughs and you have a slight Manchester accent."

"Hmm!" Andrew commented, "we will have to watch the accent although you spoke just like dear Sidney at the prison."

Charles looked at James and shrugged.

"How do you come to resemble him so closely?" he asked Jeremy.

"I have no idea. Just a weird accident of nature, I suppose," the Rabbi replied.

The five men sat round Jeremy's dining table and enjoyed a light lunch. After the initial merriment Jeremy had remembered the many happy family meals he had enjoyed round this table and this made him feel sad. However, there was much to achieve for them all and serious battles ahead before he could consider having his beloved children back with him.

Charles had been badly shaken when Jeremy first removed his beard. His memories of his father had never been happy ones and recent events had galvanised him into an even deeper dislike for Sidney. He kept looking at Jeremy and almost shuddering when he thought of what would have happened to him if the security forces had captured James and him.

They were just sipping an after lunch coffee when Martin decided to switch on his illegal mobile to quickly check for text messages. There was only one but it was of considerable length. It was from Malcolm in London and told him about Justine and most importantly about Sidney's relationship with Edgar, his son's wife. He switched off the machine and asked Charles and James to go back into the study while he discussed certain matters with Andrew and Jeremy.

"Don't worry guys," he assured them, it in no way affects you.

As soon as the two newcomers were settled in the other room, Martin told his two colleagues about the latest development.

"If we play this right," Andrew commented, "we should have both of Charleston's sons with us, against their father."

"We need to see Edgar here in Manchester. Jeremy, do you think you could imitate Sidney's voice again and order Edgar to come down here to discuss a security matter."

Jeremy sighed. "It really terrifies me doing this but it is all in a good cause. Please God, I will be able to successfully complete the task."

Once again they were forced to use Martin's mobile. Martin, had a list of the contact details for all major military bases in the country and he quickly found the number. When the operator at the Newcastle barracks answered Martin said,

"I have an important phone call for Captain Edgar Charleston from the Prime Minister. Please put him on the line." A few seconds passed and then Martin heard the clipped tones of Major Edgar Charleston.

"Yes Sir," the voice said.

""Just hold on Major, I have Colonel Charleston to speak to you."

He handed the phone to Jeremy who virtually barked down the phone in a voice and intonation identical to the Prime Minister.

"Edgar! We have a serious problem in Manchester which needs your immediate attention. This is top security; you must not mention where you are going to your CO as we suspect he may be involved in some sort of plot with his Manchester opposite number. There is a train that leaves Newcastle at 1515 hours. Make sure you are on it, my boy. You will be met at the station at 1749. Is that clear?"

So Edgar Charleston started his journey to destiny. He was a career soldier, favourite son of the Prime Minister, married to Tricia and the father of a fine little boy but only one of these attributes would remain his, after he arrived in Manchester.

Chapter Thirty seven

The Missing Son

For the first time in his life the Prime Minister was beginning to feel vulnerable. On a personal level, for all intents and purposes he had only one son, Edgar and if he was to continue his affair with his daughter-in-law Tricia, Edgar needed to be kept out of the way in Newcastle. He had thrown out his second wife Justine. As for his first wife, Daphne, she was now an old woman, as far as he was concerned. Sidney was fifty one and had no appetite for women of his own age. Justine had been good in bed but turned out to be troublesome and now Tricia was satisfying his needs and that was good for as long as it would last. As for his younger son Charles, he disgusted him. He did not know where he was, whether he was alive or dead and he did not care. He had completely disowned him.

As for friends, he had plenty of a kind but deep down he knew that they were only with him for the ride and for as long as the ride paid them handsome dividends. That applied equally to all his cabinet colleagues, the legions of civil servants that helped him to run Britain and all the other officials up and down the country. The police and army and the judiciary were totally corrupt. Most of these people had chequered pasts and as a young army officer they would never have been his associates. However, he needed people whose loyalty could be bought and that is what he had done, bought them all and used them to maintain himself in power.

Colonel Sidney Charleston sat in his bedroom brooding on all this. Who could he turn to who would give him unconditional support? He realised that there was just one person in the whole wide world who fell into this category. His son Edgar. However to call Edgar back to London would mean giving up Tricia. Anyway, he decided he could telephone him the next morning and try to have a little father and son bonding after all those years.

Sidney had an early cabinet meeting that morning. Most of these meetings had security on the agenda and today the matter was serious. The Scots were now rioting for full independence and more and more soldiers had to be despatched to do deal with this insurrection. It was 11am when he was eventually back at his desk and able to lift his private line to call his older son.

When the operator at the Newcastle barracks answered the phone, Sidney immediately asked to be connected to his son, Edgar's extension.

"He is away? What do you mean he is away?" he barked when told that Edgar was not available. "Where, the devil is he?"

The poor operator was nonplussed. "Shall I put you through to his CO Sir?" he asked.

"Yes, of course put me through to the CO!" he bellowed.

A minute later the unfortunate officer was on the phone.

"What do you mean, you don't know where he is?" Sidney bawled. "What kind of an army are you running up there? It sounds more like a hotel if officers can just come and go as they please without even telling you!"

"Would you like me to find out where he is, Sir," the hapless officer asked.

"Of course, you bloody idiot. I expect you to phone me back within fifteen minutes; fifteen minutes, do you understand?"

Needless to say Edgar could not be found. He had left the building at noon the previous day without saying a word to anyone. This was exactly what Jeremy had asked him to do but how could Sidney have known that?

"Have you checked his billet?" Sidney demanded.

"Yes, Sir. I can tell you that since walking out of here yesterday he is nowhere to be found."

Sidney slammed down the phone leaving a bewildered officer in Newcastle wondering how Captain Edgar Charleston, a good friend, could have caused him so much trouble.

Chapter Thirty eight

Brothers Converse

Edgar, now settled in a first class carriage on the Manchester train, began to think that the sudden summons from his father was somewhat strange. Still, it was definitely him, he decided. There was no mistaking that voice. It was the same voice that had terrorised his childhood and was still capable of instilling fear into him as a grown man and an army officer.

Edgar disembarked from the train at Victoria station. He saluted the soldiers and policemen as he walked through the barrier and security checks wearing his uniform. He did not know Manchester very well and hoped that whoever had been detailed to meet him would be easily identifiable. It was therefore a profound shock to be met by his brother Charles accompanied by another man. Charles was in uniform but the other man, unknown to Edgar was introduced as Major Martin Benson. He, however, was in casual civilian clothes.

"What are you doing here?" Edgar asked.

"I will tell you all about it when we arrive at our destination," his brother replied.

They then ferried Edgar round to the Metrolink platform from where there was a limited service.

"Why are we travelling on public transport?" Edgar enquired.

"Shh!" said Martin. "All will be explained soon."

They had only a short wait for a tram and after a brisk walk from the station at the other end they arrived at Jenkins Avenue. This was also a shock for

Edgar. He had been accustomed to the luxury of Downing Street for many years and before that to Mayfair. This street looked so old and tatty and had it not been for the presence of his brother, he would have suspected that the summons from his father to go to Manchester was not genuine.

They arrived at number 25, rang the bell and much to Edgar's amazement the door was opened by a Rabbi with a full beard, but there was something strangely familiar about him.

"Ah, you must be Edgar," the Rabbi said. "Please come in."

There were now six men assembled in Jeremy's small study and they sat in a tight circle around his desk.

"Firstly I need to introduce you to my colleagues. You have met Major Martin Benson and obviously your own brother," the Rabbi continued. "For now you can call me 'Rabbi' and these other two gentlemen are Andrew and James."

Edgar looked round the room mystified. If it was not for the presence of Charles he would have wondered if this was some kind of trap. However, Major Benson, although not in uniform had the look and bearing of his profession and that was reassuring.

In the circumstances it had been agreed that brother Charles would break the news to Edgar.

"Edgar," he began. "I have some very upsetting news for you of a personal nature. I am going to ask the other gentlemen to leave the room while I acquaint you with some vital information."

The other four men retired to the lounge and a very worried Edgar said,

"Well, spit it out man, is it my baby? Has something happened to my baby?"

Charles quickly shook his head. "It is nothing like that."

"Is it Mamma?" Edgar then demanded.

"No, nobody is ill or dead," Charles quickly reassured his brother.

"So, what is it?" Edgar demanded.

"Did you have any suspicion about our father's relationship with your wife?" Charles asked gently.

Edgar nodded sadly and started to talk. It was like opening the floodgates of a dam.

"I have wondered for a while if something was going on. Every time I phoned to speak to baby Julian, the little one told me that Grandfather was there. How can he have time to visit every day? He is supposed to be running the country. And then, my conversations with Tricia. When I spoke to her she was always in a hurry. It is months since we had any kind of serious communication. Even before I was posted to Newcastle I kept catching meaningful glances between Tricia and Father, when they thought I was not looking. Then when I was sent up north, I suspected that it was to get me out of the way.

"I know you are his favourite son and an army officer," he continued tearfully, "and you can do with me as you wish. As far as I am concerned he is a complete bastard. There, I have said it now! Ok, if that is treason, you can have me shot."

Charles started to laugh. "And I always thought you were his favourite son! Don't worry, you are among friends here. I was going to tell you about Father and Tricia but you already knew. What I want to ask you now is how you feel about the way he is running the country with his WDL?"

All the anger building up for months inside Edgar came to the fore and he launched into a tirade; a torrent of hatred for the way that Sidney was governing Britain.

Eventually he paused for breath and Charles was able to tell his own story and explain that there were warrants out for his arrest and that of his friend James.

Edgar explained that he had long since decided that his brother had a different sexual preference. He was only surprised that it had taken their father so long to realise this.

Charles now rose and went into the other room to ask the remaining four men to join them again. A quick nod, a thumbs up sign and a broad smile were enough to tell them that the dialogue between the brothers Charleston had gone well.

It was now Andrew's turn to 'take the chair.'

"I must tell you Edgar that we are not here to sympathise with you about your wife or Charles about the way your father has treated him. We are a serious group dedicated to removing the WDL and the Colonel from power and replacing it with a democratic government. Are you with us?"

Needless to say, both Charleston brothers pledged themselves to the struggle.

"I am now going to unveil one of our secret weapons," Andrew continued. "It is only Edgar who is not yet aware of it but he soon will be. Rabbi Jeremy, please take it off!"

Edgar was just as astonished as his brother had been and found it hard to believe that Rabbi Jeremy Pearson was not Colonel Sidney Charleston.

"It is uncanny!" he exclaimed. "Was it you who phoned me? Only you don't sound so much like him now. You have a slight Manchester accent for one thing and you speak in much softer tones."

Jeremy stood up. "Just listen to me Major. When I say jump, you jump, is that understood?"

The brothers Charleston were quite shaken.

"How did you learn to speak like that?" Charles asked.

Jeremy now resumed the far more pleasant voice of a Rabbi from Manchester.

"I spent the best part of three days listening to recordings of your father, before doing another job for Martin."

In truth, when Jeremy spoke normally, the voice was almost the same as that of the tyrant, but the volume, the words and the accent made it seem so different; so very different.

"Right we have much to do and little time to do it," Andrew said. "Let's get down to work."

Chapter Thirty nine

The Country Cottage

Malcolm's group of fifteen had been able to purchase a cottage in a small village in Hertfordshire, not far from London but somewhere considered by the WDL to be too small and insignificant to warrant the attention of the police and army. In truth, the judgement of the regime was correct about this and other similar one-street villages up and down the country. The sixty two inhabitants of Hamptonlea were all elderly and hardly a threat to the deprived way of life inflicted on the British citizens of larger towns and cities.

The cottage was in the centre of a terrace and its exterior gave the appearance of being tiny. However, like many of these homes, it stretched back into what must originally have been its garden. This was the result of a previous owner building a large extension to the rear, many years earlier.

The cottage had become an informal headquarters for Malcolm's group and was used as a refuge by any of the members who suspected they might be about to fall foul of the regime. Great care, however, had to be taken in travelling there. This involved using a circuitous route combining different forms of transport that culminated in a short train journey to the nearest larger village. A sympathiser there kept a stock of old but useable bicycles in his cellar and those wishing to visit Hamptonlea had to pedal the last two miles wearing appropriate country-style clothing. Fortunately most of those requiring shelter from the authorities were reasonably able-bodied and the two mile cycle ride was not a problem.

Malcolm told Justine about the cottage and it was agreed she would make the trip the following day. It was essential however, that Daphne should return at once to Downing Street in her old car and await further instructions.

"Couldn't you run me out there first, Daphne," Justine pleaded when she heard about the contorted journey.

Before Daphne could say a word, Malcolm interjected,

"Absolutely not! That car is far too well known. The probability is that you would lead the police or the army to the house and get yourselves arrested into the bargain."

The safe house had long since been supplied with casual clothing in a variety of sizes to suit both men and women during a sojourn there. It was, of course, simple stuff; jeans, jumpers, shirts and night-attire. All that intending residents could practically take with them were small personal items such as toothbrushes etc.

So Justine set off prepared for a long and uncomfortable journey. However, she comforted herself with the knowledge that at least she should be safe there. It was infinitely preferable to being in prison or worse.

What, in normal times would have been a drive of less than an hour took Justine six hours and she arrived in Hamptonlea quite exhausted. She was somewhat unaccustomed to the pedalling that completed her trip; indeed she had not pedalled a bicycle since her college days.

She had been given a key and she entered the house to find that she seemed to be the only resident. She was quite hungry after all her exertions and was relieved to find a fridge, freezer and larder well-stocked with a variety of food. Having satiated her appetite she climbed the stairs to find a room that was obviously unoccupied. She then unpacked her few personal belongings and checked the clothing that Malcolm had told her to expect. She was quite relieved that she would be able to live there comfortably and safely, at least for the time being. Her only immediate concern was to discover if there was someone else in occupancy and if so who? But as the days went by she remained alone in the large house. And she waited anxiously for the summons to return to London to carry out her part in the plan.

Chapter forty

Co-ordination

It was quite incredible to think that the modest house in a Manchester suburb where a Rabbi lived, had become, to all intents and purposes, a place where a vital chapter in the history of Great Britain was about to be written.

Late that afternoon, Andrew Robertson left Prestwich and returned to his home in Worsley. He had given up curfew breaking by flitting around Manchester at night. After his recent experience, he was taking no chances; especially not at this stage.

His first task was to contact Malcolm Grainger in London. Andrew still had a laptop that he had retained when the order went out that all unauthorised people must surrender their computers at the local police stations.

At that time he had taken in his old PC and when questioned he had satisfied the desk sergeant that this was his only machine. In actual fact the policeman was a long-serving member of the GMP, an honest man, who now found himself working mainly with colleagues worse than the criminals he was supposed to catch. However, the sergeant managed to maintain a low profile awaiting the day when this 'gang of crooks' as he privately described the government, would be overthrown.

Using the laptop on the internet was highly dangerous as the authorities had equipment that registered whenever an unauthorised computer was on line. The broadband connection in the house had been disconnected long ago. Fortunately he had retained a 'dongle' from the company who provided internet facilities to all official government computers. Andrew was quite terrified of using this method of communication but he now needed to speak to Malcolm urgently. He switched on the laptop and waited for it to warm-up. Next he plugged in and connected his 'dongle.' Then he activated his 'voice over internet' system. Finally he clicked on Malcolm's name.

"Hello Andrew," Malcolm answered. "What do you have to tell me?"

Andrew informed Malcolm that they now had both Charleston boys with them and that they were staying the night, together with the Benson brothers in the flat below the Rabbi's house.

"Just tell me quickly, what do you have for me?" Andrew then asked.

It was now Malcolm's turn and he gave Andrew a quick resume of what had happened with Justine.

Andrew and Malcolm then had a discussion about the next part of their plan. With this agreed, the time for action had arrived.

Andrew then waited for his wife Karen to return home from her job at a solicitor's office. She was delighted to see him. *We see so little of each other these days,* she thought, *but we are both working in different ways to see the end of this regime.*

They ate dinner together, a rarity and Andrew told Karen all the latest news. She had her own group of fifteen and was delighted that the signal had gone out to activate them the following week. Indeed, all over the country the word was being passed round from one group of fifteen to another and down the chain, that the time for action had arrived. It was critical that the vast number of people who would receive the message should all take to the streets simultaneously, not earlier and not later. It had been a long time, much longer than the original six months that had originally been envisaged, when the groups of fifteen were originally set up.

Afterwards Andrew switched on the radio. He wanted to hear the news although he knew it would only be the news that the WDL wanted them to hear. However, the item he was waiting for was there.

The Prime Minister, Colonel Sidney Charleston, will be visiting the BBC News Studios in Salford Media City, Greater Manchester on Thursday July 23rd to make an important announcement. This broadcast will take place at 3pm on national radio and will also be beamed to all officially licensed Television sets

It was time to act.

The following morning, as soon as the curfew was lifted, Andrew set out for Jeremy's house. He joined other people on their way to work and boarded a bus. He sat on the bus surveying the other passengers and wondering how many of them were in groups of fifteen and waiting for the nominated day and time to spring into action. In half an hour he was knocking on the door of number 27 Jenkins Avenue, Prestwich.

The two sets of brothers explained to him that the Rabbi was out and would soon return. In truth Jeremy, was trying desperately to look after the Synagogue and his congregants while all manner of plots and plans were being hatched in his home. He had never set out to be some kind of political activist but he had long since accepted, with resignation, that God had other ideas for him.

After half an hour Jeremy returned from morning service and the final plans were confirmed.

Jeremy was deeply worried about his part in all this and even put on his Colonel Charleston uniform as he practised his vital role in what was to happen.

Chapter Forty one

The 23rd of July 2020—A Date to Remember

For a good walker like Andrew Salford Media City was almost in his backyard. He knew he could be there from Worsley in less than half an hour. Even walking from Prestwich to Media City did not phase him but he suspected that the others may find it rather daunting. However, plans were made for each of the six men to undertake their allotted tasks on the day and to travel separately by diverse forms of transport.

Tuesday July 21st 2020....

Justine has been living a comfortable, relatively safe but lonely existence in Hamptonlea, for a over a week when she receives a message, delivered by a young man on a cycle, to return the following day, to Malcolm's flat in London. She is leaving behind relative security to prepare for her allotted task in the plan to free Britain from the yolk of a tyrant and his henchmen.

Wednesday July 22nd 2020....

*At **10.45am** Daphne climbs into her ancient car in Downing Street and set off for the Edgware Road area of London. She parks the car well away from her destination in a spot that indicates that she is going shopping on Oxford Street. (This is not an unusual occurrence.) She then walks to Malcolm Grainger's apartment just off George Street, making sure that the security services have not suddenly decided to take an interest in her movements. Malcolm welcomes her and goes over the plan with her once again. At **2.45pm** in the afternoon Justine arrives and after Malcolm has satisfied himself that she knows her part in the plan, the* *two women leave the flat, walk to Daphne's car and once again Justine has to endure the discomfort and indignity of lying behind the front seats.*

THURSDAY JULY 23ᴿᴰ 2020....

*At **9.30am** the Prime Minister, Colonel Sidney Charleston, in his Rolls Royce, is driven out of Downing street on his way to a meeting in Birmingham with the Mayor of that city.*

*At **10am** Martin Benson and Edgar Charleston in Prestwich don their army uniforms and set out to march to Salford. The sight of two officers marching along the pavements of major cities is a familiar one and will certainly not provoke any curiosity from the police or other army personnel.*

*At **11.15am** Rabbi Jeremy Pearson, complete with beard and large hat, sets out to walk towards Media City in Salford. He is accompanied by Andrew Robertson dressed in casual clothing.*

*At **11.00am** the car containing the PM arrives in Birmingham and Charleston spends half an hour with the Mayor before returning to the Rolls to continue his journey to Media City in Salford.*

*At **11.45am** Charles Charleston and James Benson dressed in business suits leave Jenkins Avenue, Prestwich to walk towards Salford. Charles is carrying a small bag. They walk slowly and appear to be enjoying the stroll as they chat and smile as they walk along.*

*At **12.30pm** Daphne Charleston, the divorced first wife of the PM, leaves her quarters in Downing Street and calls upon her daughter-in-law Tricia, ostensibly to see her grandson Julian. (This is perfectly normal.) Ten minutes after arriving she feigns illness and asks Tricia to go over to her apartment and fetch some pills that will make her feel better. Tricia rushes over to Daphne's quarters with a key,* *lets herself into the apartment where she is attacked from behind by Justine, who gags her and ties her to a chair.*

*At **1.15pm** the Prime Minister's car arrives in Albert Square Manchester where he is enthusiastically greeted by his old friend, Mayor Thomas Appleby. He takes Charleston into his office for a quick drink before they continue to Media City.*

*At **1.30pm** They are just about to leave when the telephone rings in the Mayor's office and a female voice demands to speak to the PM. It is Justine who informs her estranged husband Sidney Charleston that she has kidnapped his grandson and he will never see him again if he does not obey her instructions implicitly. He must not mention the kidnapping to a single soul and he must return at once to his office in Downing Street where further instructions will be give. If he tells anyone, other than his chauffeur, that he is returning to London, Justine will carry out her threat to steal the little boy. On no account can he tell the BBC that he will not be making the broadcast.*

*At **1.30pm** Major Martin Benson and Captain Edgar Charleston call at a limousine rental garage in Salford where a member of one of the groups of fifteen has a large Rolls Royce, identical to the one used by Charleston, ready complete with a uniformed chauffeur. They drive to the Lowry Centre.*

*At **1.45pm** Rabbi Jeremy Pearson together with Andrew Robertson enter the Men's washroom in the Lowry Centre where the Rabbi removes his false beard and changes into the uniform of a Colonel. Andrew dons a smart business suit. Martin and Edgar, dressed of course as army officers, order the centre management to clear the passages and close the shops in the area of the Men's room and the entrance where the Rolls is parked.*

At **2.15pm** *'Colonel Sidney Charleston' (Jeremy) and his bodyguard, Andrew Robertson, emerge from the Men's room and are met by two army officers, Edgar and Martin. They escort the 'PM' to his car where 'two plain clothes policemen,' Charles and James, are waiting.*

At **2.30pm** *the 'Prime Minister's' Rolls Royce drives through the security checks and open barriers up to the entrance to the BBC building in Quay house, Media City. They are welcomed there by a number of senior executives from the corporation together with the head of News and producers of the news programmes. The distinguished party then make their way to a studio where the 'PM' (Jeremy) will make his speech.*

At **3.00pm** *the news reader welcomes the Prime Minister.*

Jeremy begins his speech.

"People of Great Britain, today I have wonderful news for you. I am pleased to declare that the State of Emergency has been lifted. Obviously our streets will still need to be policed but I am herewith giving instructions that all army personnel should immediately return to their barracks to await further instructions. In addition we are reviewing many laws, particularly the laws relating to the offence of treason and we intend to restore rule by parliament as soon as a General Election can be arranged. Furthermore, the WDL is hereby disbanded and I am resigning today as your Prime Minister. All other previously registered political parties will be able to take part in the election……."

Sidney Charleston was agonising about the fate of his young grandson. At 3.05pm he switched on the car radio as the Rolls sped on its way towards London. At first he thought he was hearing a recording of a previous speech given to the nation and then he realised that, although the voice was apparently his, what was being said was nothing less than a declaration of suicide by his administration.

"Stop the car at once," he yelled to his chauffeur, Kenneth. He jammed on the brakes so violently that the police car that always followed them ran into the back of the Rolls.

Sidney was shaken up but the superior bodywork of the luxury car protected him from the worst effects of the impact. The two policemen behind, however, lay unconscious in the smoking wreck of their vehicle.

"Sorry Sir," the chauffeur stammered.

"Never mind that," Charleston bawled without a thought for the occupants of the car behind. "Get the BBC on the phone in Media City Salford."

The M1 motorway had now been closed for two years as a result of subsidence that in another age would have been long since repaired. As a result the Prime Minister's car had been making a detour through the outskirts of Northampton when the accident occurred.

It was 3.15pm by the time the chauffeur connected to the Head of News at the BBC. Sidney grabbed the phone.

"What the bloody hell is going on?"

"Who is this?" the Head of News replied and then added, "I do not like your tone. Who do you think you are speaking to?"

"Who do you think YOU are speaking to," Charleston angrily replied. "This is the Prime Minister calling. Now answer the question. What is going on there?"

"Sir the Prime Minister is here and has just finished broadcasting to the nation. Whoever you are, get off the line."

Charleston was besides himself with anger and then he saw that the whole road was filling up with huge crowds of people; men, women and children all making for the centre of Northampton and completely blocking any chance of the car continuing its journey. The Rolls was hardly the sort of vehicle that would have been observed in the outer suburbs of Northampton, even some years earlier, in a previously more prosperous Britain. Most of the crowd stared at the vehicle as they passed but with the heavily tinted windows, no one could see who the occupant was. A few people stopped to help the injured policemen but most had now developed such a strong hatred of the police under the WDL, that they just continued walking.

He sat there fuming for a few moments and then decided to phone the Chief Secretary at the Cabinet Office in London. The man was summoned and took a few minutes to come on the line.

"Ernest," Sidney demanded. "This is Sidney Charleston, I am in Northampton and surrounded by hoards of idiot people just walking towards the centre of the town."

"Who did you say you were Sir? In Northampton! That is impossible. Whoever you are, you are certainly not the Prime Minister. I have just been watching him on television."

Charleston was beginning to feel frightened. He had never been out of control before but now he was facing a situation where his own identity was in question. He glanced out of the rear window of the car and saw that the road behind was now almost clear. There were just a few stragglers still walking towards the town.

"Turn round at once, Kenneth," he ordered the chauffeur.

"Yes sir," the chauffeur meekly agreed and the car sped off to find an alternative route back to the capital.

At 3.30pm Sidney again switched on the radio. The news that greeted him filled him with a mixture of horror and amazement.

Here are the headlines, the newsreader announced:

The WDL has been disbanded at the express wish of Colonel Sidney Charleston, the leader of the party and Prime Minister. He has now resigned.

All over Britain millions of people have taken to the streets rejoicing, many with banners attacking the WDL government and Colonel Charleston.

Colonel Charleston has announced that the State of Emergency that has been in existence for over four years, has been lifted.

Troops are trying to make their way back to their barracks, having been ordered to do so by the Prime Minister himself, in a broadcast just thirty minutes ago,.

The BBC has just received a telephone call from the present leader of the Conservative Party saying that, in consultation with the leaders of Labour and Liberal Democrat parties, he will form a temporary administration to govern the country until an election can take place.

We are now going to replay a recording of the shock announcement by Colonel Charleston, just over half an hour ago……………………………………….

Kenneth the chauffeur had quickly realised that to return to London he must avoid all population areas where people were congregating. He was driving the Rolls down narrow country lanes, some scarcely wide enough for the large limousine. The journey was taking hours but at least they were moving. He had heard all the news over the car radio just a Charleston had and he was equally mystified about how the Colonel could be in his car and making the 3.00pm broadcast at the same time.

Charleston tried desperately to contact members of the cabinet and the cabinet secretary. There appeared to be a conspiracy not to speak to him and eventually he gave up and sat in the car fuming.

Eventually they reached the outer suburbs of London. It was now 9.30pm and the crowds were dispersing, returning to their homes, happy that the yolk of the WDL had been lifted from their lives. People were singing and dancing in the streets as they made their way home. They were rejoicing that the curfew had been lifted and some normality could return to their lives.

Because of the crowds it took another two hours to reach Downing Street where the policemen on the gate appeared to be completely mystified.

Charleston opened the window and recovering a little of his usual aggression said,

"Come on man, get the gate opened!"

The man in question, a police sergeant feigned surprise. He had already been told what to say when Sidney Charleston eventually arrived.

"I thought you were already inside the compound sir," he said. "I never saw you go out and I was certain it was you who came in by taxi just a couple of hours ago."

"Get the gate opened man. Call yourself a policeman. My grandson has been kidnapped and you are standing there talking nonsense."

"Sir," the policeman replied, "I can let you in but if you really are Colonel Charleston, you are no longer the Prime Minister and two of my colleagues will have to accompany you. As for your grandson, I can tell you he is safe."

"Of course I am still the Prime Minister," Charleston blustered. "Who the devil do you think you are taking to?"

"Sir, I repeat, "I can let you in, indeed there are people you will need to see in number 10, but you will be accompanied by these two constables."

As the gate sergeant finished speaking the two rear doors of the Rolls were opened and two constables climbed in on either side of the Colonel. The gates then swung opened and a bewildered Kenneth drove the limousine up to the front door of the historic building.

"Shall we go in?" one of the constables suggested and helped the now ex-Prime Minister out of the car. Then the two policemen escorted Charleston up to the door of the building.

As they approached it opened to show three young men, all smartly attired in business suits.

One of the young men stepped forward.

"My name is Peter Bertram. As the leader of the Conservatives, the largest party in parliament, with the disbandment of the WDL, Her Majesty the Queen has asked me to form a government. And this is

Jonathan Rochester the Labour party leader and William Gordon the leader of the Liberal Democrats. Until there is a general election we will all be in a coalition together."

"How dare you," Sidney bellowed, now completely out of control. "I am the Prime Minister. I have not resigned and my first duty, now I am back in London will be to have you three upstarts, imprisoned for Treason." He turned to the policemen. "Arrest these three men at once."

The response of the two police constables was to take hold of Charleston, one on each arm and then the policeman on his right said,

"I suggest you calm down sir or you will find yourself in a police cell tonight."

Peter Bertram then continued,

"Please take Mr Charleston upstairs. There are some very interesting people there for him to meet."

Chapter Forty two

Revelations

The two policemen escorted the Colonel to the entrance to a large entertaining room and opened the double doors. The room was crowded and the three party leaders who had followed Sidney up the stairs instructed the policemen to wait outside in the hallway and the four men entered the room together.

The first people he saw were three women standing together. He looked at them in amazement. His ex-wife Daphne looked at him coldly and said,

"Oh, there you are Sidney. I am afraid you have lost your job."

Justine, the woman to whom he was still legally married just nodded.

The third woman was Tricia his daughter-in-law and mistress.

"You do not need to trouble yourself about your grandson," she told him. "He is safe with me, his mother, and that is where he will remain; as far away as possible from your evil influence."

The three women who he considered sworn enemies of each other then turned their backs on him linked arms and made their way to the double doors leading out of the room.

"Let me introduce you to a few people," Bertram then suggested. He squeezed through the crowd to a group of men standing in a circle. With a profound shock Sidney realised that two of the men were his own sons.

"Edgar, Charles, I don't know what is happening here," he began. "Will you please tell these people that I am your father, Colonel Sidney Charleston, the Prime Minister."

Both young men surveyed Sidney with a look of utter disgust. Then Edgar spoke.

"Indeed you are Sidney Charleston and sadly we have to acknowledge that you are our father. You are, however, no longer Prime Minister, he is." Edgar then turned to Peter Bertram, smiling a sad little smile. "As for your military title, I don't think it will be much use to you when you stand before a military tribunal to be stripped of all your honours."

Sidney was outraged. He turned to his younger son Charles. "Are you also turning your back on me after all I have done for you?"

"What you have done for me? All you have done for me has been to make my life a misery and you would have murdered my friend James Benson if you had the chance."

Sidney suddenly reverted to type.

"You and your so-called friend disgust me. You are both perverts. You need wiping off the face of the earth."

Sidney turned with a start as he then heard a strangely familiar voice addressing him from behind.

"I do not think that is a nice way to talk to any human being, let alone your own son!"

He turned round to find himself facing a Rabbi wearing a large black hat and navy suit. He was the same height as Sidney and sported a full black beard as is customary among most Jewish 'men of the cloth.'

Even now Sidney had the arrogance to argue.

"I thought you people didn't agree with gays," he said, his eyes blazing.

"That is not a topic for conversation," the Rabbi continued. "Suffice it to say that, unlike you, I would never demean another human being, especially in public."

Sidney swung round again to turn his back on the Rabbi. Then he recognised Major Martin Benson standing next to another tall fair haired man.

"Captain Benson, what the devil is going on here?"

"I am afraid the game is up," Martin replied. "You, Mr Charleston have run this country into the ground for your own benefit and that of your friends. And this gentleman here is Andrew Robertson. He is one of the team of fine men who will be helping this country to recover. I don't think he likes you very much as you were directly responsible for the death of his elder brother Sir James Robertson, Chief Constable of Greater Manchester."

Sidney was beginning to realise the predicament he was now in. He was in Downing street but instead of being among friends and cronies he was in the midst of his enemies.

Then Sidney felt a gentle tap on the shoulders. It was the Rabbi again.

"I would very much like to talk to you in private," he said.

"Can we go in to the office over there," he continued pointing to a door that led to the vacant office of one of the permanent secretaries of state.

"Rabbi," Sidney replied. "I do not know what you can want with me. I am trying to defend myself from these men who have unjustly turned on me. I have no time for religious chit-chat." He turned his back on the Rabbi again and was irritated to feel yet another tap on his shoulders.

"Now what do you want with me," he said as he swung round. Then his jaw dropped in utter astonishment. Jeremy had removed his hat and false beard and Sidney Charleston found himself staring into what was, to all intents and purposes, his own face.

"Now will you follow me into that office?" the man who no longer looked so Rabbinical asked.

As they made their way through the crowd there were many comments. They were all senior activists from the groups of fifteen and they knew all about Jeremy's strong resemblance to Charleston. However, to see these two men, physically so much alike and in character so different, crossing the room together was quite uncanny.

Once inside the office Sidney turned to Jeremy.

"So you are not a Rabbi after all. Who the hell are you?"

"I most certainly am a Rabbi," Jeremy explained. "I had no desire to become involved in any of this sorry business but, for obvious reasons, no one could impersonate you like me."

"But how come we look so much alike?" Sidney demanded.

"I have no idea and although I do not condone embarrassing people in public, on our own I have no hesitation in telling you that I consider you to be one of the most evil men I have ever had the misfortunate to meet."

Anyone speaking to Colonel Charleston in such a manner up to just a few hours ago would have been carted off to jail and would almost certainly have met with a fatal accident within just a few days of arriving there.

Instead Sidney seemed to crumple and he dropped backwards into a nearby chair.

"So who are you?" Sidney demanded wearily.

"I told you, I am a Rabbi. My full name is Rabbi Jeremy Pearson."

"When and where were you born?" Sidney asked.

"I was apparently born in Brixton in 1969," Jeremy answered. "I say apparently because I was adopted and the details of my birth and parentage do not go beyond that information. And you, where and when were you born?"

Sidney nodded. "I have exactly the same information."

"I have had the advantage, if I can call it that, of knowing about you and your uncanny physical resemblance to me for some time," Jeremy continued. "It is perfectly obvious that we are twins." Then he bethought himself. "Do you have any object at all that might have been a possession of our real mother."

Just then there was a knock on the office door and two policemen entered.

"Which of you is Sidney Charleston?" one of them demanded.

Sidney was still in his uniform as a Colonel in the British army. He rose from the chair and with all the dignity he could muster he said,

"I am Colonel Sidney Charleston, Prime Minister of Great Britain."

The policemen continued, "Sidney Charleston I am arresting you on a large number of serious charges including conspiracy to murder. You have the right to remain silent......"

Then Jeremy interjected and addressing the policeman he said, "Could we please have another five minutes before you take him away?"

The constable nodded and gestured to his colleague to leave the room.

Sidney knew that the gigantic project of hijacking Britain was now over. He had thoroughly enjoyed the power and now he must pay the price for his misdeeds. He turned to his twin brother and said,

"There is nothing they can do to me that will make me regret for one minute, everything I have done."

"Only God can forgive you but as for me, your soldiers robbed me of the wife I loved and for that and the countless other acts of evil you perpetrated, I can never forgive you," Jeremy replied.

Sidney began to laugh hysterically. "I really do not care if your God forgives me or not. I enjoyed every minute of it and I ask forgiveness from no one."

He pushed his hand into the inside pocket of his jacket. For a fleeting second Jeremy thought he was going to take out a pistol but instead be brought out a tiny package. He carried it over to the desk and feverishly opened it.

"Here," he shouted, "here is the keepsake that I was left by my mother."

Jeremy knew exactly what he was going to see and pulled a similar tiny package from his pocket.

Inside the two packages were identical metal charms of the type that were often hung on bracelets when silver and gold were beyond the budget. These charms were in the shape of seven branch candelabrums.

But further startling revelations about their origin were to appear just a few months later from a totally unexpected source.

At 1.15am the gathering at 10 Downing Street dispersed. By now Sidney Charleston, the tyrannical ruler of Britain for nearly five years, was securely locked up in a police cell to await the sort of fair trial he had denied his many victims.

Peter Bertram, the leader of the Conservatives, the new Prime Minister, at least until after a general election and his colleagues, Jonathan Rochester of the Labour party and William Gordon the leader of the Liberal Democrats retired to the cabinet office in the same building to face the overwhelming burden of work the new government had to undertake, to put Britain back on track. The country had been raped and the scars would sadly linger for many years.

Chapter Forty three

The Aftermath

Little by little, the country was emerging from the darkness of the Charleston tyranny. It would be a slow process but Britain would emerge stronger in the knowledge of how easily democracy, if not protected, can be used to destroy it's very self.

Her Majesty the Queen and the other members of the royal family recommenced their duties to the nation that Charleston had treated so grievously.

Rabbi Jeremy Pearson returned to his congregation in Manchester to a heroes welcome. His children were brought back to him by his parents-in-law. They told him that they hoped and prayed that eventually he would find a suitable lady with whom to settle down again. They knew, of course that he could never replace their daughter but life must go on. He re-grew his beard and from that day he devoted himself solely to the spiritual and physical welfare of his community.

In the general election the following year, Andrew Robertson was elected Labour member for Salford while Malcolm Grainger became Conservative member of Parliament for the Mayfair constituency. Despite their divergent political interests they remained good and close friends.

Major Edgar Charleston resumed his career in the army as did Captain Martin Benson but to defend Britain against it's enemies not to attack their own people.

Chapter Forty four

The final disclosure

The new government had instantly set about restoring all normal methods of travel and communication. It was therefore something of a surprise when the doorbell at the Rabbi's house rang at 10.30pm one evening, just a month after the tumultuous events at Downing street.

Who can this be? Jeremy wondered. *My phone service has been completely restored. Thank heaven, there is no longer a curfew. So why creep around at this time of night?*

The Rabbi peeped through the spy hole on the door and saw a frail looking old man standing on the doorstep.

He opened the door.

"Can I help you?" Jeremy said.

"My name is Jack Rodgers," the old man said. "May I come in. I have some very interesting information for you."

"It is rather late," Jeremy replied. "Can you not make an appointment to see me tomorrow?"

The old man looked crestfallen.

"I have only just arrived from London. I did not realise how long it would take me to get here."

The Rabbi relented.

"Well, you had better come in. Can I get you a hot drink?"

The Rabbi escorted the man into the study. In the stronger light of the halogen bulbs he could see that this man was indeed, a very good age.

As soon as the visitor was sitting comfortably, sipping his hot coffee Jeremy felt able to ask him the purpose of the visit.

"As I mentioned before at the front door, my name is Jack Rodgers," the old man explained. "Does that name mean anything to you?"

"No, I can't say it does," the Rabbi replied.

"I am ninety one years old," he continued. "I used to live in Brixton, south London."

Jeremy nodded, suddenly becoming more interested with the mention of the London district.

"I saw your story on television last week," Jack explained. "And I saw that you're twin is that accursed rascal Sidney Charleston."

"Yes," Jeremy answered. "So why are you here?"

"It was me and my ex-wife Julie who found you," he continued.

Jeremy was overjoyed. Now, out of the blue, after all the years of searching and wondering, here was someone who knew at least something about his origin.

"How do you mean 'found you?'" Jeremy asked.

Jack Rodgers then recounted the story of the twins birth in great detail even mentioning the television programme that they had been watching when they heard the cries of the young mother in the alleyway behind their home.

Jeremy listened patiently and then gently enquired,

"Did you know the name of my mother?"

This question seemed to cause the old man some problem. He became somewhat agitated and sat there staring at Jeremy before deciding to continue.

"What I have to tell you now is not known to another living soul. I have children, grandchildren and great-grandchildren and I want you to promise, as a man of God, that you will never divulge any of this to any living person. I am going to die soon and I do not want my children to think ill of me when I am gone."

"From what you have told me so far," Jeremy commented, "you have nothing to be ashamed of. You and Mrs Rodgers were the heroes of the story."

"You said 'so far' and you are right," Jack continued. "However, what will you think of me when you hear the rest of the story?"

Jeremy was intrigued. What family secret was this old man about to recount?

Jack took a deep breath and continued. "Your mother was called Helen Gold. She was from a Jewish family over in Cricklewood. She was seventeen years old and working as a trainee manager in a small supermarket in Brixton owned by her parents. She became friendly, very friendly with a married assistant manager at work, an older man, and one thing led to another and she became pregnant."

At this stage the old man began to cry.

"When she told this assistant manager that she was expecting his baby he wanted nothing more to do with her. She then told her parents that she was pregnant and they threw her out. They said she had disgraced the family and in those days that sort of thing did not happen to nice middle-class Jewish girls from Cricklewood. After that I did not know what happened to her."

He gave Jeremy a searching look.

"The only thing I do know was that it turned out she was having twins, and she was looking for me when she went into labour!

Jeremy gasped, suddenly realising the implications. "So are you saying to me that you are my father?"

"Yes, yes, I was the assistant manager," Jack replied tearfully, "and also, I now know, the father of the most hated man in this country, Sidney Charleston."

Jeremy sat there for a few minutes in shock. He looked at the old man in wonder; *could this really be the father he had sought.* Then another thought occurred to him. No wonder he was so attracted to Judaism; his mother was Jewish so he had been Jewish from birth.

The old man had nowhere to go that night and Jeremy offered him a bed in his home. He did not like Jack very much but he was a human being in need of shelter. By his own admission he was indirectly responsible for the death of Jeremy's mother and that crime could not be his to forgive.

The night was a sleepless one for Rabbi Jeremy. He tossed and turned as he considered the implications of Jack Rodger's story.

It sounded as if his mother had been an innocent, naïve young girl who had been taken advantage of by an older married man. Jeremy prayed, somewhat unnecessarily that he may be spared from inheriting the genes of his father, now lying in the next room. He knew nothing of the rest of Jack's life but he did know someone who would seemed to have inherited those genes and made a far, far worse job of living a decent life, even than his father; his twin Sidney Charleston, the British tyrant.

Six months later the Colonel was sentenced to life imprisonment with instructions from the judge that he should never be released. However, just four months later, without ever learning the story of his birth, he died, of a heart attack, in prison.

The End